Fools Trade

TJ Arant

Contents

"He's mad that trusts in the tameness of a wolf, a horse's health, . . . or a whore's oath."

*King Lea*r (III, vi, 19-21)

Chapter 1

Anson Sayers looked across the desk at me. His gray eyes bored like a frozen laser into mine. Cold but meaningful. "How do you feel about the police academy, Jackson?" Typical shrink question. Not leading anywhere.

"I was invited. I guess I feel... invited?"

"Do you feel special? Does the invitation imply anything like that?"

I didn't feel special. Any more special than I'd felt in the jungle in Vietnam. I was there not because I was special but to do a job. "It's a job."

"Some might say that it's a special job. One that's difficult to do." As usual, Anson was doodling on a notepad in his lap. Even when he looked at me, he seemed to be drawing, like an artist savant who didn't need to look at the pad to create something.

I corrected him. "Difficult to do right." Any damn fool can wear a shield. Lots of damn fools did.

"Still." He sketched at something. "The feeling must be a good one. An important part of society has invited you in, has said that they want you to be a part of them. Yes?" More circles. More lines. "Do you feel validated in some sense?"

To be honest, I didn't know how I felt about it at all. Detective Bobby Flood had greased the skids. He knew someone who knew someone. I was ex-military. I didn't have a record. I had a college degree. And I'd been in on three prominent busts that Metro had missed. Two they'd missed because they were lazy. One they'd missed because they didn't care.

Flood believed it was skill, that I had a talent.

"Luck," said the monster inside my head. Right place, right time. Nothing more than that.

Anson was my therapist. I'd started seeing him because I had stopped drinking so much, but I hadn't stopped being the person who needed to drink. Battle fatigue, some called it. Shell shock.

All I knew was that the nightmares kept coming. Loud noises still shot me through the roof. Everything in the world, anything in the world, made me hypervigilant, ready to spring.

Or ready to run.

And I wasn't getting any better. Drinking through the day didn't help, and I'd given it plenty of time. I didn't want to try something stronger, like drugs. Or something different, like losing my mind. So I was trying therapy.

Anson was good at letting the silence happen. All I could hear was his pencil scratching on the notepad.

Finally, I spoke. "I may not make it through the academy."

"It can't be harder than basic training was." I imagined his pencil making bombs, blowing everything sky high. "What's so hard about it?"

It wasn't the physical training. It wasn't the weapons instruction. I'd even abandoned my post-enlistment dread of firearms and bought a couple for myself. It wasn't the driving or the ethics or the intricacies of patrolling. All those things had analogues in the army, and Anson was right, there wasn't anything in the academy that was as hard as combat, even if the instructors would have you believe that it was combat out on the streets every night. Or could be.

No, I hated the return to a chain of command. Vietnam had demonstrated that the chain of command was a chain made to strangle the enlisted man. Out in the bush, leading a squad, I had some small measure of control, of flexibility, but get me in a situation where an officer was around, and I was always one smart-ass comment from the stockade.

Being a cop, starting at the bottom of a rigorously hierarchical organization, was likely a recipe for failure. Eventually.

I could see it already in my academy class. I was one of the best in all the curriculum elements. I had a four-year degree. I excelled in firearms. Despite my old Impala, I also finished top of class in emergency operation of vehicles. And combat had done one thing in spades: it made me someone who aced all the practical exercises. Once you have been shot at for real, everything else seems easy. Or at least predictable.

My mouth finally opened. "What's hard is taking orders."

"Is that a problem for you? You've taken orders before, haven't you?"

"This is different, Anson. This is taking orders when I'm used to being on my own. When I'm content to do my own thing."

He raised his eyebrows and softened his eyes so they didn't bore in on me. "Isn't that the reason for the order of command? So that the work can be done safely and effectively?"

"Maybe. Or maybe it's just one big clusterfuck. Like the Army."

He moved his gaze back to his notepad. "Sounds like you'll need to decide quickly. That attitude won't get you far in the police force."

***

Anson wasn't wrong. I was two-thirds through the police academy when the decision was temporarily postponed for me. I fell during a practical exercise.

No, that's not right.

Our team was working with a fire academy team on a fire emergency drill. I had to assist with evacuating the building. As I moved with a dummy in a carrying maneuver, one of my classmates barreled into me, causing my ankle to bend in a way it's not engineered to bend.

It got to be the size of a lemon. Then it got painful. Then the lemon got purple. All in the span of an hour.

My ankle wasn't broken, but the orthopedist at Vanderbilt said the sprain was bad. "Worse than a break, really. You'll feel the effects longer, for sure." No heavy duty for three weeks. To start with.

"Three weeks, huh?" My academy leader, a crusty salt named Clark, raised his eyebrows. "Too bad. You're so close."

"What's it mean, Boss?"

"It means you'll have to sit it out and start over in the next group." He thumbed through a clipboard. "Are you paying your own way, or have we already promised you a spot?"

That was the deal. If your spot was secured, Metro paid the freight. If you didn't have a job yet, you were on the hook for the tuition. Whether you got through it or not.

"Metro's paying."

"All right. I hope you have a way to cover your bills in the meantime. Looks like you won't draw a paycheck from the city for a while."

It was just fine. I had a free apartment. I had an understanding bartender and restaurant. It'd worked for a couple of years before Metro came calling. It'd work again. "I'll be okay."

To be honest, the sprain had come at the right time. I'd already chafed under the direction of officers who knew less about physical conditioning, weapons, and vehicles than I did. Yes, I had a lot to learn about policing and laws, but I found that my old distaste for idiots telling me what to do was still intact, even though I was nearly eight years out of the Army.

Some people aren't meant to take orders. Or give them, either.

And I had left Anson's office pretty much resigned. The next academy class didn't start for another three months, so I had plenty of time to figure out how to tell them to stuff it. In the meantime, I needed to find a short-term gig, one that didn't put too much stress on my gimp ankle.

So I took myself, lock, stock, and bum leg, to Hannigan's. Hannigan's used to be my office, at least before somebody got the bright idea that I could be a cop.

It was a place where I could be found, just like any office. No one answered the phone for me unless somebody rang the pay phone in the corner. The wait staff knew me, and they had no trouble anticipating my needs, just like any good secretary would. Katie knew when it was time to bring a cheeseburger. Charlie knew when it was time to bring a bourbon. Life was good. Life was calm. Life was relatively cheap, or at least the bill could be delayed.

I guess it was not that much of a surprise when Parker Street showed up and sat in my booth.

Street was a tall man, around six-four, and he had the sort of complexion that told you he spent time outside. That might surprise you, since he was a vice president at a big insurance company downtown. But I knew he spent a good bit of his weekend time at the hunt club, riding horses and chasing foxes.

And I knew Parker Street because he had hired me a year ago to follow his son Jamison, a Vanderbilt undergraduate who chased foxes of an entirely different sort. I had found young Jamison in the clutches of a notorious Nashville femme fatale and had managed to extricate him from a situation that would've been entirely embarrassing to his father. Parker Street had paid me handsomely for that.

He was about to tell me why he was back in my office. I ordered a beer, more out of habit than anything.

"It's like this, Trade." He was moving his hands back and forth, as if to punctuate his sentence. "There's a missing jockey. It's not a good situation."

I figured the hunt club was all about guys riding their own horses. "What does a missing jockey have to do with anything?"

"You know the Nashville Steeplechase, don't you?"

"Sure. Horse race. Rich people. Kind of a second-rate Kentucky Derby for the Harpeth Ridge set."

"Horse race, yes. Kentucky Derby, no. That's a race on the flat. The Sweepstakes is a steeplechase. Whole different kettle of fish."

"All right. Different kind of race. Same swanky set. Same ladies in hats and men in pastel coats." I'd seen the pictures in the paper. Not my kind of crowd.

Jamison settled into the booth, his eyes a little wider. "Fair enough. But one of the jockeys, the rider for a horse called Fool's Trade, is missing. And Fool's Trade is the odds-on favorite to win, just like he did last year."

"Maybe he's gone off with his girlfriend." It'd been known to happen. Even happened to me once or twice. "I mean the jockey. Not the horse."

Street ignored my humor. "Look, Trade, the Steeplechase has always been a kind of local affair. Sure, there's lots of money on the line, but most of the people involved have the kind of disposable income that just makes it a lot of fun. For years, the riders have been local folks. I'm too large, but sometimes it's even been the owners of the horses themselves who rode. It's not the sort of thing that gets people all riled up."

"Then why are you riled up?"

"I'm riled up because the whole thing is getting out of hand. Michael Martin, Fool's Trade's owner, brought in a big-time British jockey. His name is Richard Banks. Why's he done it? He intends to win. And Banks is the jockey who's missing."

So much for the leaving-town-with-the-girlfriend angle. "But the horse won last year, you said."

"That's right. The kid who rode Fool's Trade last year, the son of the horse's trainer, has decided he's not riding anymore. And Martin insists that he's going to win. If you want to know the truth, I think he was replacing the kid anyway, and the kid got wind of it."

"Why all the drama? I mean, if it's just fun and games for you guys?"

"The rumor is he's got money trouble. And whatever you say about fun and games, the winning purse is up there. Thousands." Katie had brought Parker an iced tea, and he finished half of it in one gulp.

"Why would the jockey take off, then?"

He shook his head and polished off the rest of the tea. "Most of the club is unamused with Martin. Bringing in a professional jockey goes against the grain. People don't like it."

"And you suspect your rich friends of kidnapping? That makes almost no sense at all."

If you wanted to know the truth, in my mind, rich people were perfectly capable of such things. I didn't know many of them, but I knew enough about them to suspect that they were rich, at least partly, because they were willing to do whatever it took to protect their own interests. If that meant kidnapping a jockey and hiding him out until after a horse race, well, I guessed that was par for the course. But even among the Harpeth Ridge bunch, it was hard to think there'd be one who'd kidnap a jockey over a local horse race.

"So what do you want me to do about it?"

He looked at me and my half-finished beer. There was just a trace of disapproval in his eyes and maybe more than a trace of distaste. I didn't look like much, truth be told. The flannel shirt I wore was an old one, and my jeans and cowboy boots contrasted unfavorably, in his mind I'm sure, with his Brooks Brothers outfit. Still, I had done a good job for him once, and he thought I could do a good job again. And I still had my spiffy short haircut, courtesy of the Nashville Metro Police.

"I'll pay you five hundred a week, plus whatever expenses you incur, to find Richard Banks."

I sat up straight. That was a lot of money. It was enough money to make up for the corresponding distaste I had for Street and his pals.

"And if I find this jockey, a bonus?"

He smiled. "If you find the jockey, I have little doubt that Michael Martin will add to the kitty. For now, though, five hundred a week plus expenses." He smiled again, this time a little more like a shark. "Do we have a deal?"

I didn't have to think long or hard. Five hundred dollars for a week of work, plus whatever I could eat and drink in that period, was a deal I didn't get often. Hell, it was a deal I never got.

I smiled back. "Sure, Parker. Let me see what I can do."

Chapter 2

It was too early in the afternoon to be sweating in a car seat. But here I was, outside the Harpeth Ridge Country Club, sitting in a beat-up and past-its-prime Chevy Impala, smoking a cigarette, and waiting to see if anyone cared that I'd been waiting for fifteen minutes.

I'd taken some care about my appearance. Navy blazer, banker's gray dress pants, and a fresh white shirt. I'd even rooted through the bottom of my closet and come up with a navy-and-gold-striped tie that, if you didn't look too closely, might pass for Saville Row. I had shaved, and I still had the neat, sidewall haircut they'd given me at the police academy, though thankfully, the sidewalls had grown in, and I was just neat rather than stupid-looking. The cane I limped on was the stupid-looking part.

The country club appeared to be what it was: a refuge for people who had more money than they knew what to do with and no inclination to care what you thought about it. The main building had the feel of the real Tara, the one of Scarlett and Rhett fame. The windows had plantation shutters on the inside and storm shutters on the outside so that they could resist storms of both natural and unnatural varieties. The doors to the front entrance were black and heavy and made to withstand whatever force could be mounted in an assault. Even the portico, with its railing and piping, seemed to communicate a kind of arsenal mentality, as if it had been made so that archers or riflemen could appear and face down any attack.

In short, it looked like a Southern plantation, but one that had learned the lessons of the late lamented War of Northern Aggression and had no intention of being surprised again.

At long last, a superior-looking doorman took pity on me and admitted me into the sanctum but not before pointing me to the employee parking lot behind the kitchen. He didn't seem to think my car belonged where the members and their guests parked, and maybe he was right. Parked among the cooks' and porters' cars, the Impala fit right in,

I parked in the back and came back around front, and my navy blazer and gray slacks were admitted as if there was nothing at all wrong with me, the way I looked, or what I was there to do. Inside, a black man in an uncomfortable-looking outfit of black suit and starched collar nodded to me and pointed toward another black man, this one wearing a shirt that was equally starched and a coat that was equally black but decorated with golden shoulder cords, signifying, I suppose, that he was further up in the rankings.

"If you'll follow me," he said. His voice had the barest hint of a well-cultivated but still false foreign accent, vaguely British but also vague enough to have been something else. If it was meant to convey that even a servant, in this world of wealth, was superior to me, it worked.

I didn't belong here.

"Wait here," he said, opening and then closing an interior door.

While I waited, a woman, about twenty years old and wearing a tight-fitting jacket and a pair of riding breeches, walked up to me. Actually, she slinked but not quite in the way the girls down on Lower Broadway did. Her slinking was more the kind that told you she could be interested, but interested like you were some knickknack she was thinking of buying.

She was a blonde and wore her hair back in a ponytail. It probably looked nice when it was allowed to fall on her shoulders, which you could see in the tight jacket were the sort of finely shaped bone structure more suited to being costumed as a rider than to actually being one.

Still, the clothes looked good on her. And who cared if she could ride a horse? She looked like she enjoyed the part.

"You're new here." She moistened her lips just a little with her tongue.

"How can you tell? Maybe I've been around before."

She had green eyes that looked me up and down, as if looking at my gray pants might help her determine if I was new or not. "You're not bad looking."

"All depends on your type, I guess."

"Who are you?"

"Theophilus J. Luke. The J is for Jackson."

She slinked a little to my other side, as if she might squeeze the melon just to see how fresh it was. "What kind of name is that?"

"New Testament, I think."

She moistened her lips again and gave me a smile. I know the type. With the Lower Broadway girls, it's supposed to part me from my money. With her and all her money, I don't know what it's supposed to make me part with. I could imagine, though.

When it didn't do whatever it was supposed to do, she gave me a pout. "Do you ride?"

"Not me. I'm here to see Michael Martin."

Her eyes narrowed. If she had tried to be seductive or something like it before, now she seemed to want me to be afraid. She breathed loudly through her nose. "What do you have to do with Daddy?"

"He called me, so I guess that is his business and mine."

She slapped my arm with an open hand. It was a silly movement. I barely felt it. But it seemed to be important to her. So much that she did it again. When she started to do it a third time, I caught her in mid-slap. "Let me go, you bastard."

"I don't know what your deal is, but you don't impress me."

"I'll tell Daddy. He protects his Abbie."

"What you tell him is your business, sister."

"You're a beast." She pulled her wrist out of my hand and thought about slapping my arm again. "I'll find out anyway."

"No doubt you will. But not from me."

I was shown inside a room that could fairly be described as Colonial Plantation. Shutters on the insides of the windows, their louvers tilted so that the sun reflected up without making the room warmer. A couple of leather loungers with opulent ottomans. A mahogany side table for each as the set flanked a small fireplace with an ornate mantel. It was not a large room, but it gave off the scent of money.

A man sat in one chair. He was silver haired, and his complexion was ginger, the sort that doesn't do well in the sun. Or rather, the sort whose complexion turned from freckled to one large freckle, giving the appearance of a tan. He wore a houndstooth sport coat and khaki slacks with a pink polo shirt. I put him in his mid-seventies, but he could have been a decade either way. Any victories he had were hard-won, and from the looks of him, they'd taken their toll.

He held a glass in his hand. The glass held bourbon.

"Are you Michael Martin?"

"You've set Parker Street aflame." His smile hardened, and he took a sip.

"If Parker's on fire, it's not my match that lit him up." I looked from him to the woman in the other chair. "He came to me."

The woman shifted, crossing her legs in the other direction. She looked as if she had come in from riding. She wore riding pants and long boots still, though the boots were cleaner than you'd expect if she had been near a barn. She was older than Daddy's Girl outside but not by a whole lot. She was also a lot better looking.

"I don't know why you consented to this." She lit a cigarette and looked over her shoulder toward him. "It's none of Parker's business." She glanced toward me and blew smoke dismissively. "And it's certainly none of his."

I was beginning to feel unwelcome all over again. "If you'd like me to leave while you two talk this over..."

Martin took another sip, the frozen smile still on his face. "Imogene was just leaving. Weren't you, dear?"

There was a long moment where I didn't know if she was ignoring him, thinking, or getting ready to slug him. At last, however, she stood up. "I'll be in the bar." Her walk, as she strode away, was athletic and precise. The sort I could see on a winner, walking to the awards stand.

Martin didn't look that much like a winner. The smile had left his face, replaced by a thin-lined grimace. What had once been dimples on either side of his mouth were wide indentations like little slash marks, the kind you tally when there are already four you've counted. The slash across makes five.

He motioned toward the seat. It was still warm when I sat.

"Drink?"

I shook my head.

He poured a little more for himself from a carafe on his table. "Parker filled you in, I take it?"

I told him the little I knew. "I'm supposed to find Banks. That's my bottom line. I don't know what the top line is or what's in between."

"The top line is that Fool's Trade must win the Sweepstakes."

"That's why you brought in the professional jockey."

"Correct." He took another sip. The slashes on his face grew deeper.

"And I understand that's not a popular choice here at the club?"

"My friends here at Harpeth Ridge are a little provincial. Stuck in their own insignificant version of a piddly little past. They don't like outsiders."

I could feel that breeze when it blew. "Your wife among them, it would seem."

He sighed. "Imogene doesn't care much for the club either. Don't take it personally. I think she only really cares about horse people. Jockeys, for instance." He finished the last of the drink and set it on the coaster that protected the table. "Why did you come to me? Parker Street has hired you. Without consulting me."

I didn't get the problem. Street was primarily concerned about the club, but he was also trying to help Martin. "You don't want help finding Banks?"

"I'm a rich man. I don't need others taking on my work."

"If you want to hire your own man, please feel free." I didn't want him to feel too free. Five hundred a day plus expenses was too good a deal.

His eyes were blurred. Maybe he'd been in the seat a little too long, a little too close to the bottle.

"I've got other problems." He reached into the inner pocket of his jacket. He took out a folded piece of paper and handed it to me. "Read it."

Inside the piece of paper was a business card that read, "Quintile Racing. J. Farley, Owner and Proprietor."

I raised my eyebrows, questioning.

"Look at the paper," he said.

On it was written, "Mr. Martin. I've enclosed the copies of wagers that have been placed on the Sweepstakes. If our positions were reversed, I would want you to let me know."

On the other side of the paper was a series of notations, all of which indicated that over $50,000 had been placed against Fool's Trade. Some of the action had been placed by R. Cameron. The rest, the main part, had been placed by R. Banks.

I handed the papers back to Martin. "Doesn't look kosher to me. Who's Farley?"

"He's a bookie. Quintile Racing is just his front. But you're right about this being wrong all the way around. You can't have a jockey betting against his own horse."

"Who's Cameron?"

"Well, there's a point. If I had hired you, I would have told you to start with Rex Cameron."

I considered whether this might be the way Michael Martin had gotten rich in the first place, by letting others pick up his tab. "Who's Rex Cameron?"

He looked up, surprised. "Rex Cameron. Of Cameron Industries." When I showed no recognition, his face slanted. "You really don't know much, do you?"

I made my face as blank as I could. If I said what I was really thinking, I probably would have been thrown out of the country club. "I don't run in your circles."

"Well, you would have to be *non compos mentis* not to know the Camerons. They are Nashville royalty. Well, business royalty, anyway. Rex is the young scion, the latest branch. A little rough around the edges for my tastes, but he'll even out, I suppose."

"Why should I start with him?"

"Word is, they had an argument. Banks and Rex. That's the rumor, anyway. And given what's on that paper, they both bet against my horse. Banks's horse, too. If I consider it along with what I know, it looks suspicious. Anyway, that's the rumor. They argued."

"Why is it just a rumor?" As far as I knew, rumors were rumors and facts were facts. They rarely intersected.

"You really don't know much, do you? Rumors are the raw materials of the truth."

"Where I come from, rumors are lies. Usually."

He refilled his glass and held it aloft. "Welcome to Harpeth Ridge. Where we are all just rumors. And if I am right about Mr. Farley, he's offering to keep a rumor quiet if I come up with the right amount of cash."

"And?"

"And I'd like you to take care of it." He drank his bourbon like medicine, made a face, then frowned at the empty glass. "Yes. Investigate it. Take care of it."

"What about Banks?"

"Parker hired you for that. If you find him, you find him. Imogene would be pleased, I imagine. But I'll double what he's paying you, and that puts me at the head of the line. You do my job first." Now he frowned at me like I was an empty glass. "Understood?"

I saluted. I didn't take orders well, but I took money like a champ. "You got it. Anything else?"

He let his frown relax, but it never made it to a smile. "No. Follow the rumor, find the truth. Take care of Mr. Farley's problem." The grimace settled. "Take care of my problem."

"You mean pay him off, if that's what he wants."

Finally, the grimace straightened, and he smiled. "Even if that's not quite what he wants. I will leave the disposition of the matter in your hands, Mr. Trade."

Chapter 3

SINCE I WAS ALREADY at the country club, I went looking for Rex Cameron. He had ridden in the last four Nashville Sweepstakes and had done well. Not so well that anybody thought of him as a pro rider. But he had taken care of Daddy's investment and performed well enough.

He wasn't hard to find. All I had to do was ask one person, a man standing in the lobby. He pointed. "Hear that racket over there? Just follow the noise. That's our boy Rex."

I followed the sound of the voice. It was angry as it rose and fell then rose again until it was a near scream. "Listen, little brown man. If I want your wise-ass platitudes, I'll put in an order for them, okay?"

The young man to whom this was directed was clearly a staff member at the country club. He was a short, skinny boy of indeterminate age and nonwhite parentage. He looked as if he might cry.

"And if I ever hear you talk to me that way again. I will have you fired."

The young man scattered as quickly as he could without appearing to run.

The author of this diatribe stood about five feet seven inches tall. He was strapping without being wide, athletic without showing muscle. He had a thick head of dirty-blond hair parted on the side that came across his forehead in the style that was current. He wore a green polo shirt with the ubiquitous alligator and a navy blazer sporting the Harpeth Ridge club crest on the breast pocket. He wore khakis and topsiders. All in all, he looked like what he was. An entitled rich boy.

He turned and saw me. Our eyes met, I didn't waver, and he didn't either. "So? What's your problem?"

I guess I didn't look like I belonged there. Otherwise, he wouldn't have said that in the tone he did. "I just followed your voice. If you are Rex Cameron, I'm looking for you."

"I'm Rex Cameron all right. Who the hell are you?"

He was no better mannered with me that he was with the staff member. But that was fine. Even leaning on a cane, I was half a foot taller and outweighed him by about sixty pounds. Plus, I knew how to take care of myself, even if I don't usually get physical. What I usually do is take it until I don't have to take it anymore and then, like I said, six inches and sixty pounds make a difference.

"I'm interested in hearing about your conversation with the jockey from England."

"We didn't have a conversation. I told him what he needed to know." He sneered. "He's an idiot."

"Sure, I get that. I'm sure that you know much more than he does about the horses here and the steeplechase course. What I'm interested in is why you would get in a fight over that. Did he start something?"

"Nobody started anything." Cameron smirked. His lip was curled, although that could have been a natural condition brought on by too much money and too little talent. But it was without a doubt the sort of face that he used on everyone, and in most cases, he probably got away with it.

I watched him to make sure he wasn't going to elaborate, and then I said, "Usually, people don't get into loud disagreements unless there's something at stake. What's at stake here? Maybe the fact that you don't like a pro jockey coming in. Maybe it's something else?"

"New jockeys don't bother me. There's always room for someone who's learning the trade. But pro jockeys? That's a whole different story. This is a gentleman's game. If you bring in people from the outside, people who don't belong here, everything we do becomes different. And what we do is special." He lowered his tone as if talking to a child. "But you wouldn't understand that."

I decided to take his bait. "I can see your point. I really do. But somebody has disappeared, and it's somebody you had an argument with."

"What in the hell is that to you?"

"I've been asked to look into it."

"Are you a cop? Because if you're a cop ..."

I didn't tell him that I was still officially at the academy. I didn't tell him that someone asked me unofficially to investigate it. There was no need to say any of that. I certainly didn't tell him I knew about his bets.

Plus, I had a feeling that Metro might not like somebody in the academy branching out on his own. In fact, I knew they wouldn't. It was basically a subset of an entire morning of training a few weeks ago.

I just looked at him in what I considered my best Clint Eastwood High Plains drifter stare. Probably would have worked better if I hadn't shaved. Maybe I would have looked a little more like Clint.

"Look, buddy. I don't really need your garbage. As far as I can tell, you are a rich boy who's got too much time on his hands and too much attitude for his own good. If I need to, I can wipe the floor with you.

"But I'm not doing that. I'm just asking a couple of questions. Let's try again." I walked closer, leaned over him, and got as intimidating as I could, given the cane. "What were you arguing with the jockey about?"

He stood his ground, leaned back, and looked me in the eye. He jutted out his weak jaw. "I'm a member here. I can have you removed."

"Do what you need to, but I'm asking you a question. If you want me to go and talk to someone in management about this question, I can do that. But I think you'd rather just answer a simple interrogatory." I smiled. Maybe it was a Clint Eastwood kind of smile. I hoped he could hear the winds blowing through the High Plains. "Let's keep it simple and easy."

"Like I said, we didn't have an argument. I just told him he wasn't welcome, and I told him the way things were."

"And what did he say?"

"He said that he didn't work for me, so he didn't much care."

"And then?"

"And then we went on our way." Cameron had the kind of blue eyes that make you think of Nordic people. Or of well-bred, snotty, prep-school kids. Right now, those eyes were angry slits, and he looked like he really wouldn't mind calling someone and having me removed from the grounds.

I stood looking at him. "That's fine, Cameron. When a jockey goes missing, everybody has questions. The next people asking questions may not be as nice as I am. They might have badges, and they might have access to jails." I sort of wished I had a small cigar to complete the Clint effect. "You'd do well to answer their questions in a more friendly way than you answered mine. If you don't get your attitude under control? I wouldn't be surprised if you don't get asked downtown."

"We'll see about that. In fact, I have lawyers who will see about that."

And with that, he turned and began to walk away. After four or five steps, though, he turned, looked back at me, and said, "I didn't get your name."

"No. You didn't."

He laughed. It was a condescending laugh. "Okay. I see how it is. I'll find out who you are. And you best believe that will not be a good thing for you."

"Sonny, I doubt anything you say or do will have much effect on me. But if it does? You'd be well advised to know I'll get the last word."

He shrugged, shook his head dismissively, and then looked reasonably certain of himself. "Okay. We'll play it that way. But you should not cross me. Whatever your name is."

Through the window, I watched him saunter to the parking lot, jump into a sweet little TR-6, gun the engine, and leave like he had important places to be. Right down to the sports car, he was what he was.

I couldn't stand him.

Chapter 4

My ankle throbbed from standing too long, and it wasn't getting better. I left Cameron, turned left, and found myself in a big room. A big room with a high ceiling, the kind that will either make you feel really important or really small.

It all depended on how you felt about yourself, I guess. My opinion was that it was too big and too high and didn't have much to do with me one way or another.

The windows opened out on manicured grounds, and the sunlight was bright, abnormally so for an April day. Enormous satin drapes framed the windows, and their persimmon shimmer didn't go with springtime. They were more like autumn. Maybe they'd change them. It was the sort of place that could afford to.

Imogene Martin had adjusted herself on a white chair so that she was displayed to her best advantage, if best advantage meant that I could get an unobstructed view of her long legs encased in clinging pants and supple brown riding boots. She was long without being especially tall, and her shoulders were wide enough to tell you she had a good bit of strength. Her shoulder-length hair was black and curled the way that only a curling iron makes. But she'd done a good job of it. Or someone had. It was easy to see what Martin and Banks saw in her.

I certainly saw it. If she wasn't already married, I'd have given more than a thought to a different kind of conversation.

She didn't invite me to sit. My ankle damned her for it. It wasn't interested in how attractive she was.

She had a drink, a different one from the one before. She sipped it, looked at me over the rim of the glass.

"Are you really a detective?" Another sip. "You don't look much like the type. A little too young." Another sip. "Don't take this the wrong way. You look a little immature for what Michael is wanting."

I could have told her that all my immaturity was left rotting in a jungle in Southeast Asia, but I let it go. If she was trying to get a rise out of me, she would have to wait.

"Did you like Michael?"

"Enough. How much do I have to like him?"

"I suppose he told you about Banks."

"Sure."

"Banks is a real dandy. You know, the sort whose stuff doesn't stink."

"Uh-huh."

"He didn't make a good impression, you know."

"I wasn't aware he'd made an impression at all." According to her husband, Banks had at least made an impression on Imogene. "But then, I'm just getting up to speed."

She gave a little shrug. "Oh, he's been around long enough. Several of the owners have met him. Parker, of course. And Rex Cameron."

"Yes, I know about Rex. Seems like his stuff doesn't stink either. Or do I have that wrong?"

She finished her drink and put the glass on a small silver tray. She readjusted herself so that I got the full length of those legs from a different angle. "Do you think you can find Banks?"

"Who knows? I'm getting paid whether I do or not. It'd be easier all around if your husband just reported it to Metro."

"Michael may do that, in fact." She watched me with those gray eyes, framed by that black hair. We were silent while a man with white gloves and a subservient look entered, took her drink, and paused in front of her. She shook her head no, and he left. "What's your next step?"

"When's the last time anyone saw Banks?"

"How should I know? Didn't Michael say?"

I grinned and shook my head, shrugged my shoulders.

She bared her teeth just a little, the way small animals do. "You're pretty full of yourself, mister," she snapped. "And as far as I can tell, you have little enough reason to be."

"That's right. As far as you can tell." I began to limp toward the door of the too-big room with the too-high ceilings. "And as far as I can tell, there's no harm in letting you preen a little in your comfy chair there. I saw the legs. They're damn nice." I chuckled. "As far as I can tell."

She jumped to her feet, the gray eyes and black hair now nicely complemented by a fine rose-colored flush rising in her cheeks. "No one talks to Imogene Martin like that."

I laughed out loud. "That's curable, you know."

"What's curable?"

"Talking about yourself in the third person." I had my hand on the doorknob.

"Wait." The color was still in her cheeks, but it was subsiding. "Sit down."

I didn't move.

"Please."

We both sat. This time, she didn't bother much about the angles of her legs. She didn't have to. They were still nice. Even my ankle approved.

"Banks had been here three weeks when he disappeared. The last time I saw him, he was at the hunt club."

"That's not here at Harpeth Ridge, right?"

"No. It's south of here. The country club is a private club. The hunt club is exclusive. Just a few of us own the property, unlike here."

"And you had a lovely little dinner and drink with Banks?" Her husband seemed to think there might have been a little more. A little "alone time" at the very least.

"As I said, he is full of himself. Insufferable, if you want to know the truth. But he and Michael were of one mind about the sweepstakes."

"All in to win it?"

"Precisely. Michael is paying him a good bit for that result."

"Hope he's worth it, then." Imogene didn't seem to know that Banks had multiple ways to get the payday he wanted.

I left her and the big room. I walked down a path that indicated it led to the stables. I consulted my ankle and didn't follow the path. Soon enough, I would.

An April storm was coming. The sky behind the trees was a dark, mottled brown, and the wind picked up. I could hear the rumble of thunder, and there was a first and then a second flash of sheet lightning. I could taste the coming rain in the back of my sinuses, a kind of damp and persistent tickle.

I didn't like anyone I'd met. Imogene Martin had a nice presentation, but I bet she was hell on wheels and, besides, she was married. Daddy's Girl was bright and shiny, but she likely had the same trouble as all her kind, which boiled down to rich and oblivious. Martin was a drunk, and Cameron was a jerk.

And Banks? The missing jockey looked for all the world like a man who would bet against his own interests. He was going to make it pay off, no matter what happened.

Maybe he was betting on his own charm with the ladies too. Even if they thought he was insufferable.

Chapter 5

THE STALLS WERE CLEAN, a surprising clean if you were raised on a farm and were accustomed to barn smells like I was. When I grew up, the barn was a place where the smells of feed, silage, dust, and pollen all mixed with manure, the ammonia from urine, and the smell of whatever animals were in the barn at any given time. Mules had a certain ambiance that was different from cattle. And if your barn was connected to a hog lot, that brought a whole different olfactory sensation.

But these stalls were clean because they housed animals whose value was far greater. The stalls were cleaned once daily, at a minimum. The barn had huge fans beneath the line of the roof, and they pulled air out and forced fresh air in through the double doors, which were open at each end of the barn.

The lesser barns, where the lesser horses bivouacked, didn't have the whole-barn system but instead had box fans bungee-corded on the front of the stalls, meant to pull air out from the stall.

And this barn, where the best of the best were housed, had both a whole-barn system and individual stall fans. Each stall had a solid front, four feet up, then an upper portion that was open so the air could feed outward. Each of the four stalls on the east side of the barn, the ones with the fronts facing south, had an attached walk-in run separated from the stall by a door with windows. Each stall had a heat distribution system, one that included electrical heating coils that could be activated when the night temperatures got chilly.

These horses had it better than any of our animals when I was growing up. In fact, they had it better than some families I had known, at least as far as comfort was concerned. Some of those families lived in houses that had one outlet per room. These stalls were fully wired. And as far as their worth in the marketplace? Yeah, the horses probably won there too.

Willie Peele was the lord and master of these premises.

He was the sort of man who was used to getting his own way. Maybe that was what it was like when you were around horses all the time.

Willie Peele looked like he was getting his way every day, all the time.

He was a short man. He wore faded dungarees, barn boots, a faded Western-style checked shirt, and a cowboy hat twice as big as his head. He moved precisely. Each move was measured. The sort of man who never put a foot down without knowing where it would land.

I knew someone like him once. My father, who never seemed in a hurry but never stopped moving. That sort of deliberate motion was the sort of thing I grew up with and got used to. Maybe I even inherited a little bit of that. It was gone now. Vietnam ensured that.

But it was certainly a fact that you couldn't speed my father up, and you couldn't slow him down. He was, in some ways, a relentless force. In other ways, he was an infuriating drag.

I had the feeling Willie Peele was just that way, too.

"I don't know what it is you're looking for, mister, but I reckon it ain't none of your business anyway." He put down the brush he was using to clear the horse's back of any grit it may have picked up in the night. He picked up a sponge and gently stroked the hair even flatter if that was possible.

"I'm working for a man who disagrees. He believes something has happened to Mr. Banks."

"If there has or hasn't, it ain't none of my worry. Nobody asked him here. And I don't have any concern for him."

"Well, someone did ask him here, and you know who it is. It's your boss. Michael Martin."

"I reckon that's true enough. But hiring a rider is just one part of this operation. Might even be the least important part." He reached behind him to grab the saddle blanket and carefully folded it in half. He placed the blanket on the horse's back, positioning it forward over the withers and sliding it back into place.

"You believe the most important part is the trainer."

"You know anything about horses?"

I nodded. "Some."

"If you know about horses, then you know that the rider and the trainer have to be of the same mind. This boy he brought in, this British boy, he and I don't share a single thought. Much less a whole mind."

"You think Martin made a mistake bringing him in?"

"I don't know about mistakes. I don't make them myself." He hooked the offside stirrup over the horn and folded the girth cinch back over the saddle seat. He then lifted the saddle high and brought it down gently on the horse. It was so softly done that it barely made a sound.

The horse was a bay with a beautiful shine on his coat. The sort of horse you see and are immediately reminded of equine magnificence. Horses always made me think of how insignificant humans are. Horses are not smart, don't get me wrong. In their natural state, they are nowhere near as smart as cattle and fall far down the line from hogs.

No, horses are not smart, but they are magnificent. And Fool's Trade was a magnificent horse.

"Do you think that Banks and you will get to where you need to get? It'd be a shame, after all the trouble Martin took to bring him here, if you and Banks couldn't coexist."

"All it takes is for him to change his mind." Willie Peele finished the ministrations of saddling the magnificent beast. "That's all it takes," he said. "Just has to come around to my way of thinking."

"What can you tell me about Rex Cameron?"

He spat. "What do you want to know? Rich boy. Rides a lot. Knows how to handle a horse, I reckon."

"Would you be surprised if I told you that he and Banks had an argument?"

"Nothing surprises me about Cameron. He's a nasty little son of a bitch. Like I say, though, knows his way around horses. Especially that little filly of his, Jet Pack."

The phrase "nasty little son of a bitch" combined with the phrase "knows his way around horses" probably could apply to Willie Peele too. "He's a good rider? How many times has he won the Sweepstakes?"

If I expected a smile, I didn't get one. "Lots of people haven't won a Sweepstakes. That doesn't make them bad riders. It just means they haven't won. There's been times I haven't won."

"Has your son Bob won?" I knew the answer to that already.

"Bob is a good horseman. One day, he'll be a good trainer." That was all he had to say on the matter.

I was getting nowhere fast with Willie. Like my father, he had nothing to say unless he had something to say. And he didn't trust me enough to have anything to say.

"If you think of anything, you can reach me here." I handed him a card. It had my name and phone number, with the phrase, "Leave a Message."

He looked at it briefly and flicked it on the floor next to the horse. "If you're around tomorrow, you'll find that you're still not welcome around here. I don't care who hired you. I won't be needing your card because I won't be calling you. Now, if you're done here, you can skedaddle."

"I've got no problem with that, Mr. Peele. But you may be surprised. Later on, you might want to talk to me. I have that effect on people sometimes."

I turned and walked slowly out of the barn. One foot after another. Just like my daddy would have.

Chapter 6

THE PHONE BOOK HAD only one Quintile, and it wasn't followed by Racing. In fact, it wasn't followed by anything, leaving it to the imagination of the phone directory user to intuit what business Quintile was in.

When I dialed the phone number next to it, I got the recording that said it was not in service.

I drove the Impala over to Thirteenth Avenue North and parked at an oblique angle to the address in the phone book. It was the sort of mixed-use block you see everywhere downtown these days. Here, a little light industrial, maybe somebody running a two- or three-man machine shop operation, would be next to somebody who'd set up shop as a brake-and-tire guy, the sort who would cut you a better deal than the Firestone dealer would. Next to that would be a pawn shop and, if you were in the right part of town, a barber shop or a beauty shop. You'd have a whole block of small businesses, none of them synergistic with any of the others but just regular folk trying to make a living as small business owners.

And that's what Quintile was too, I supposed. The sign out front said, "Travel Agent," but there was no self-respecting traveler making plans in this place. The front windows were dusty and not well taken care of, and the storefront looked more in keeping with the grease monkey next door than with someone who could take you to exotic climates.

I knew if it was a bookie's place, they might take you to the cleaners, but not to Tahiti.

I lost the tie and the jacket, then took my time walking up to the door, trying to see if I was being watched. The street was empty for the time of day, but it might have been empty all the time. Thirteenth North was not exactly a destination spot, halfway between downtown and northside.

I turned the knob at Quintile's and felt the wood door catch on the metal below. Somebody a long time ago had felt that rub and neglected to sand the door or to replace the doorjamb. As I shut it, a faint lifting of dust tried to get in my nose and make me sneeze. I resisted.

The place could have used a dusting all around. My eyes adjusted to the light, and I could see that the space was sparsely furnished. Here and there were random wooden chairs, the kind that your Aunt Tilly got rid of when she bought the new dinette set. Toward the back was a metal desk that someone had found at the army surplus. I knew because I had seen enough of them when I clerked at Fort Carson, where they stuck me for the months left in my enlistment after Vietnam.

On it, the desk had a blotter, a phone, and a redhead. She was by far the most interesting of the three.

"You want something?" She wore a brown lace-through top that contrasted nicely with her red hair. Her skirt was one of those tie-dye jobs, but this was no homemade affair. It was stitched nicely, edged in white fringe, and had a slit up the side. Along the slit, I could see that her tanned legs were encased in cowboy boots. By the looks of them, the boots cost more than the rest of the outfit, but that's the way it goes in Nashville.

I made myself smaller and less intelligent. I had pulled my hair forward, as if I didn't have a comb at home. I leaned on my cane. "I'd like to discuss a trip to the south of France. You see, my Aunt Tilly has just died and left me her estate."

She popped the gum she chewed. "What?"

"This is a travel agency, isn't it?" I pointed to the window. "That's what it says."

She hopped off the desk. "Sure. I mean, of course."

"I'd really like to cross the ocean on a ship. Always been a dream of mine. Besides," I whispered, "airplanes give me the willies."

She shook the skirt and feathered the fringe. "I'm not really the person to talk to about that. Mr. Farley..." She stopped and looked each way like someone crossing a street for the first time. "Mr. Farley is the travel agent."

"May I see him, then?"

She looked each way again. Something about the street bothered her. "No, Mr. Farley is away."

"I'm happy to wait." I smiled, hooked the cane on my arm, and stuffed my hands in my pockets. "Is it okay if I wait? He won't be long, will he?"

"I'm not sure." She exhaled then seemed to have crossed whatever street was in her mind. "He could be very late."

I grabbed one of the old wooden dinette chairs. "Perfect. I'll just wait here for him, then." I sat as if eager to see when Farley would get there.

I didn't know what I expected, but I was sure that a bookie joint wouldn't call the cops because some dope thought he was in a travel agency.

And I was right. The woman went back to the desk, sat down, and fiddled with a pencil and a legal pad. From sitting in with Anson, I could have deduced she was doodling, but she could have been writing in little, angry letters.

Once or twice, she looked at me. When I looked back, she smiled. Sort of.

After about fifteen minutes of this charade, a man in a twill suit entered, nodded to me, then proceeded to the desk as if I wasn't there. With their heads together, the woman and the man buzzed back and forth. I couldn't make out the words, but I could make out the tone. They were having a conversation familiar to each of them.

After a sixty-second conference, the woman reached under the desk and extracted a briefcase. The man gestured a "thank you" with his head, a kind of brisk and definitive snap forward, and took the brief-case. He left the way he came.

"You know," I said, rising, "Mr. Farley could be very late."

"I am sure he will be."

"In that case, I'll come back tomorrow. Will he be here in the morning?"

The woman practically purred. I think she was pleased I was leaving. "Most definitely." She went back to her work, whatever it was. "You'll know him. He wears one of those English hats."

"A bowler?"

"Yeah. That's what it's called."

I touched my forehead in salute. "Then that's when I'll return. I can't wait to plan my trip to France." I slid toward the doorway, leaning on the cane. "Aunt Tilly would be so pleased."

Outside, I did the look-each-way thing myself. Looking south, I saw the man ambling with the briefcase as if he had all the time in the world. I crossed the street and jumped into the Impala to wait.

He pitched the briefcase into the open passenger window of a newer model Plymouth and climbed in the driver's side. We got our engines humming at about the same time, and I let him get down the street before I pulled out to follow him.

Tailing people in Nashville's downtown is hard. Which is to say that it's too easy. Most times of day, there's just not enough traffic to give you cover, so you have to be content with being too far away or right up on the guy's bumper.

Either way, it doesn't matter. Nobody thinks they're being tailed in Nashville. The dishonest think they know everybody who might tail them, and it would never occur to the honest folks that they could be tailed at all.

Whether this guy was honest or dishonest was anybody's guess, but I stayed with him until he got north of Father Ryan High School. He turned up a hill in the Sylvan Heights neighborhood, nice enough but not high rent like the country club set. He stopped in front of a two-story white house with a wraparound porch. He got out with the briefcase, walked to the front door, and left the briefcase right in front. Then he retraced his steps, got in the Plymouth, and drove off.

While I decided whether to pick up the tail again, the screen door opened. I couldn't see who was there, but I had the distinct impression that a man picked up the briefcase and closed the door.

Clearly, I needed to know who was on the other side of that door. And what was in the briefcase.

But I could guess what was in the briefcase.

Chapter 7

I DROVE BACK DOWN the hill toward Elliston Place, hung a right on Charlotte, and parked the Impala. The sky was grayer and more threatening, but I walked down the street to the nearest pay phone. I took Farley's card out, put a dime in the slot, and dialed the number on his card. Nothing. Just like the nothing at Quintile.

I guessed that Farley wasn't the kind of man to do his kind of business on the phone.

I walked another block to the only bookie joint I knew. This one was fronted by a dry cleaner, and it had the advantage of doing a business taking in dry cleaning.

It was a front for the Dixie Mafia.

People might have heard about them with the *Walking Tall* movies and the Buford Pusser mess out in west Tennessee. And yes, that was Dixie Mafia stuff. The west Tennessee kind. But there was more to them than that, which you could say called out its failures because it got so much press.

Real Dixie Mafia was nothing like the real mafia at all. And, except in west Tennessee, it never would have wasted its time getting into a pissing contest with a county sheriff.

Dixie Mafia, in fact, was a very loose confederation of thieves, hoods, and hustlers. They involved themselves in everything from illegal booze to contraband cigarettes to drugs. The more hardcore of them were into prostitution and everything that connects to that, including pornography. And in the heart of all that action is the real action: call it gambling.

The Nashville branch was headed up by a guy named James Lee Penny. He'd been a horse trainer to start with, but he'd long ago moved into more profitable lanes of business. If it was illegal in Nashville, you could bet James Lee Penny either controlled it or allowed it to happen.

My question was whether Farley was one he controlled or one he tolerated. That would make a lot of difference in the way I handled the matter for Michael Martin.

The man at the front counter had a rooster tail that would not stay down, even though it was ninety degrees in the shop and every thread he wore was soaked through with sweat. That rooster tail just stood tall, as if nothing could bring it to heel. "Ticket?" His shirt said his name was Ed.

"Nah, Ed, I'm not picking up or dropping off. I'm looking for the manager."

"If you got a problem with our work, you could tell me."

"Nothing like that, bud." I popped a cigarette in my mouth but didn't light it. "I got a business proposition." I looked toward the back, where I suspected the manager might be. "If you know what I mean."

"Sure. You in the dry-cleaning business?" He wiped the sweat off his face. "Or you in another line?"

"I have several lines, but none of them are press and starch, if you know what I mean."

He knew. "See that gate? Let yourself in, go straight back, and turn left after you get past the steam irons. She's back there."

I did as the man said and came to a door that said the manager had an office there. I knocked, and the door flew open. "I thought I said..."

I smiled. "I'm sorry. I wasn't here when you said whatever you said." Sometimes, people respond to a smile and an apology, even if they don't know you.

"Oh. I thought it was Ed."

She wore sandals and jeans that she'd rolled up to mid-calf. Her blouse was sleeveless and unbuttoned at the top, and she had brown hair that matched her brown eyes. Some women have eyes that challenge you with their intelligence, a kind of purposeful repudiation of whatever you thought about them. She had those eyes, and she likely didn't take any crap from anybody.

"I have a little problem, and I'm hoping you can help me." I smiled again. Her eyes didn't. "It's not a dry-cleaning problem."

"Then what makes you think I can help you?"

I gave her my card. She looked at it and handed it back to me. "Who are you?"

"Jackson Trade. Like the card says."

"If that's supposed to mean something to me, it doesn't." The eyes were beginning to look impatient.

"I'm working for a man who's in a jam." She didn't change her expression. "It's about some bets somebody has made. Bets on a horse."

"And you come to a dry cleaner?"

I looked over my shoulder. "Can we talk in your office? I'll be brief."

"Yeah, fine." She stepped aside so I could enter. "But you better be done in two minutes. Otherwise, I holler out front and get somebody to help you leave."

"Just like any other dry cleaner would." I smiled again. "Right?"

She shut the door. "All right, darlin', what's your deal?"

"I'm working for a well-known man in town, a guy who owns a racehorse. A guy named Farley is squeezing him over some bets a couple of other guys made. I told him I'd take care of it."

"Yeah?"

"Listen, lady, I'm not an idiot. I know that your boss runs a lot of the book in town. If Farley is one of yours, I'll have a quiet talk and see what we can work out. If Farley's freelance, though..."

"You'll take another path, so to speak?"

"If he's not one of Mr. Penny's associates, I will reconsider my approach. That's why I'm here."

She reached past me and took a pack of Virginia Slims, shook one out, and lit it by bending a match from a paper matchbook and igniting it with her thumb. I've seen guys in bars try that, and almost none of them can get it right. Not the first time. Usually not any time.

"But who are you, Jackson Trade? Are you freelance too?"

"I don't work for any of Mr. Penny's associates. If I did, you'd have heard of me."

"Not always true. You could be from Mississippi. Or Georgia. The organization has a lot of men I don't know."

"I'm local. And I'm not connected. Just an honest guy trying to do honest work."

She snorted cigarette smoke out both her nose and her mouth. "Honey, there's not three honest men in this town, and none of them ever came in here. But you're right about one thing."

I could smell a faint trace of floral scent in all that cigarette smoke. Somehow, the fragrance merged with the tobacco, making it sweet and hard at the same time. "What's that?"

"You should probably take a different approach with this Farley character. I never heard of him either."

Chapter 8

It rained like Biblical times. Too fast, too much, no Ark, and no Noah in sight. The rain filled the ditches and ran down the street in small waves. People who had umbrellas found them useless, and those who didn't have umbrellas got soaked, which meant that everybody felt the rain down to their Fruit of the Looms.

It was six in the evening. I was sitting in the Impala and wishing for the days I kept a pint of cheap bourbon in the glove compartment, just to keep warm when I needed to. Given that the Impala's windows didn't seal tightly enough to stand up to a rain like this, it would have been nice to have something to take the chill off.

It served me right. I had come back to the place where the man in the twill suit had dropped the case, hoping to find something out. What I hoped for was anyone's guess.

People tended to think I knew what I was doing more than I really did. Most of my success came from sitting on my ass and watching who did or did not show up. And then asking the ones who did show up what the hell they thought they were doing.

It wasn't scientific and it sure wasn't like police work. But, like a blind squirrel, every so often, I came up with a nut.

After ninety minutes or so of waiting in the rain, I figured this squirrel was going to make me work for his nut.

Finally, two cars crested the hill behind me. One was a nice Mustang, one that looked like it could blow you off the starting line. The other was a turquoise Lincoln Mark V, the kind with the fake spare tire relief on the trunk lid and the little round opera window cut into the vinyl roof. They're massive, but a certain type of driver likes them. The kind that likes fake tires and little round windows, I guessed.

The Lincoln parked, and the Mustang double parked with it. From where I sat, I couldn't see who got out of the Mustang, but I could easily see who got out of the driver's side. A short man wearing a bowler hat. It had to be Farley. Who else in Nashville even had a bowler hat?

The rain came down in buckets, and I could almost feel the water flow underneath the floorboard. The sheets of rain, combined with the growing condensation on my windshield, kept me from seeing much.

I waited until the traffic had died down, opened my door, and shot my umbrella at the sky. I zigged down the street then zagged back. Still, no one stirred, either on the street or in the house. When I got even with the passenger side of the Mustang, I crouched and pulled the door open. The rain got between my umbrella and my back and drenched me. While it did that, though, I opened the glove box and checked the registration. Imogene Martin.

So that was one way to have some fun. Hang out with the bookie who's handling inside bets against your husband's horse.

I shut the car door, zagged then zigged back, and sat in the Impala. I was too wet. I was too sober. And I was going to wait to see what happened next.

It took another thirty minutes to happen.

I heard the sharp report of gunfire, the kind that a semiautomatic makes when its owner has business on his mind. There was a kind of muddied sound, half scream and half moan. Then I heard the roar of an engine from the back side of the house. Whoever had been there had parked a street away and had run through a yard or two to get there.

I considered whether I should peel out in pursuit but thought better of it. I wasn't likely to catch the other car, not in an old, oil-burning Impala. Besides, since Imogene was in there with Farley, it would be a nasty thing if I could get them help but didn't.

I jumped the hedge and tried the front door. Nothing. I sidled close to the house and slunk to the side, where I could peer through the window. I didn't see much, and what I saw only threw shadows. The back door, where the intruder had been, was flung open, and I went in. The French doors' curtains were whipping in the rain, and I untangled myself from them.

Farley's body lay on the floor, a bright red hole in his shirt, matching the one through his neck.

Imogene lay on the couch, naked as the day she was born. She didn't have a red hole anywhere. But she was no more conscious than Farley.

When I checked, though, she was breathing. That was more than I could say for him.

I searched and found her clothes behind the couch. She was a load to move. I didn't bother with the hose and the underwear; that would have been too time-consuming to get on her in her current state, even if I could have been successful. I managed to get her skirt pulled up and zipped, then I got her raincoat on her, arms through the correct places, and knotted the belt so that she was presentable, after a fashion. I slipped her pumps on her feet, stuffed her underwear and blouse in the raincoat's pockets, and hoisted her up on my shoulder. My ankle screamed like it had a needle stuck through the bone.

Her purse held the Mustang's key. I pitched her in the back of the car, got in the front seat, and fired up the V-8.

It was a good bet that I wouldn't take her home to Martin, even if I knew where they lived. I did the only reasonable thing. I drove out to Harpeth Ridge.

Once I was there, I managed to scare up the night porter, who seemed to do more sleeping than watching on the night shift. "I need some help here, buddy." I had my hand on the back of his collar. I was dangerously close to raising him to his feet using only that. "Where's your boss?"

His face told me he didn't relish the prospect of getting him out of whatever place he was.

"I need him. Now."

Five minutes later, the impenetrable gaze of the boss, gold cords and all, gave me a hard look.

"Come with me. You'll see why."

Once outside, I opened the Mustang's passenger door and pushed the front seat forward. Imogene was still there. She was still out of it.

He wrinkled his nose. "Is she drunk?"

"I have no idea, I assure you."

"Then what …"

"I found her in a place she shouldn't have been. In a bad way. Drunk? Drugged? I don't know. But she couldn't stay where she was. Police were on the way." I didn't want to tell him too much. But I wanted him to understand.

Fortunately, his discretion took over. "I see." He motioned to the night porter. "Let's get Mrs. Martin's things and convey her to the overnight guest quarters." He made sure the man understood with a stern look. "You stay here," he said to me. "I'll be back."

When he returned, he had a slightly softer face but still one with an edge to it. "I won't ask any more questions. I don't want to know the answers. But I do want to thank you for your discretion."

"No need to drag anybody through the newspapers, right?"

"Indeed." He looked behind me. "That is Mrs. Martin's vehicle?"

"Yep. It didn't need to be where it was, either."

"Then I assume yours is still where you left it."

"That's right. So, if you could call me a taxi. . ." I leaned hard on the cane.

"Consider it done, Mr. . . ."

"Trade. You can call me Jackson."

He raised himself to his full height. "I will call you a cab, Mr. Trade. If you will wait here."

I waited. I still wasn't welcome inside the club. It didn't matter.

I had the taxi take me close enough to Farley's house, and I hobbled the rest of the way, half the time forgetting how to put the weight on the cane so that I didn't hurt. When I got there, there was nothing happening around the house. No cops. No ambulance. Nothing.

I figured they'd come soon enough. I got in my car and drove home.

It was two hours and a couple of solid belts of bourbon before I could close my eyes. And another belt and thirty minutes more before I went to sleep. And even then, my ankle was singing the blues.

Chapter 9

It had been a dark and stormy night, but the morning after was all sweetness and light. The birds sang. The sun shone. Everything was clear.

Which meant that I had to squint to see anything, and the birds were too damn loud. I felt hungover. I was losing my touch. Two cups of strong coffee made no difference to my headache or my mood.

If I had a pair of sunglasses, I would have worn them indoors.

I went through *The Tennessean* twice but didn't find any notice of the problems at Farley's house. Not that I expected anything regarding Imogene. But I figured that the Metro boys had to know about the dead body. Maybe they were keeping it quiet.

I was about to shower my headache with some soap and water when the phone rang. It was Bobby Flood.

"How's your bum leg?"

"It has a hangover. My whole body has one."

"You should take better care of yourself." He laughed one of those one-note laughs, the kind that aren't laughs at all. The kind that are judgmental and dismissive at the same time. "People say you've been busy. That true?"

"Jeez, Flood. It's barely nine."

"And you've got a hangover. I just thought you might like to come clean. You know? A guy who's supposed to be at the academy? And taking on extra work?" He clicked his tongue. "Not the right thing to do."

I didn't know if he knew about Street. Or Martin. Or both. Hell, you never knew what Flood might know. "I get asked to do things, Flood. You know how it is. Rich folks have problems too."

"Stuff seems to happen with these rich folks. A hot little Triumph TR-6 went through the pilings at the river last night."

I waited. I didn't even clear my throat.

"You know anyone with a car like that?" Flood was bright, all sweetness and light. "There's a guy inside it."

I exhaled. Slowly. I hoped I did it silently. "I might."

"Thought you might. How about I swing by and get you? We can run over there together, and maybe you can ID the body."

I did the best I could with a third cup of coffee, a shower, and a shave. By the time I was presentable, Flood was standing on my doorstep in his gray polyester suit.

"You can't afford a decent suit?" His service holster bulged unattractively.

He looked at me. Jeans. Flannel shirt. Beat-up Tony Lamas. A belt buckle that said, "Nothing Runs Like a Deere."

"I don't take fashion advice from farm boys."

It was a brisk drive to the river if there was no traffic, but this morning, the Church Street traffic was snarled because there was construction at Ninth. Flood cut across and barreled down Jefferson until he got closer to First, then he drove like a bat out of hell to the river.

We got out. "You could just put the bubble on top and let the siren rip."

He put a fresh toothpick in his mouth. "What fun would that be?" He peered toward the river. "There she blows."

He pointed to a winch that had pulled a blue sports car up onto the shore. The car glistened in the sunlight, the winch's chains still around it. It wore a large round ding on its driver's-side door and a mashed front end. We made our way down the unpaved, grassy riverbank.

Flood and I gave it the once over. The driver was still in his seat but had fallen over into the passenger side, as if some angry giant had slapped him and he'd stayed where he had landed. His neck was bluish, which matched the Izod polo he wore. It didn't match a raised reddish knot on the side of his head.

Flood turned to the man handling the winch. "What you got?"

"He came down the old Cement Plant Road over there," he said, motioning with one of those Popeye the Sailor arms. "Looks like he lost control and left the street. I'd say he got airborne, since we found him way out in the river."

"Lost control? Sounds like a bad accident to have. No idea why he'd be running so hot on a little street down here."

The winch operator spat. "I said he lost control. Didn't say he didn't mean to."

Flood's toothpick wiggled. "What the hell's that mean, bud?"

"He could lose control on purpose. Wouldn't be the first time somebody used the river to kill himself."

"Maybe he was drunk." Flood knelt briefly near the bank, tossed his toothpick in the river, and looked at me. "What do you think?"

I shrugged. "Who knows?" I looked at the guy with the Popeye arms. "What do you think?"

"A man who's driving that car, that fast, down here? He's suicidal, whether he knows it or not."

Flood and I retraced our steps to his car. We leaned against it as we watched the ambulance arrive and the men load the body into the back. They would take the body downtown, and the medical examiner would check him out. No matter what he found, though, he wouldn't be able to tell us what was in his mind. That would either take good police work or a message from the Almighty.

Flood fished a fresh toothpick from his pocket. "Know him?"

"Yep." I let the air rest between us for a second. "Rex Cameron."

Flood didn't startle easily. Or at least he didn't show it. "Rex Cameron of the Nashville Camerons?"

"That's the one."

He nodded and stuck the toothpick in his mouth. While he talked, it attached itself to his lower lip and wiggled as he spoke. "Looks like I need to talk to a family member, then. You know any of them? You could come along. Make it easier."

I didn't know any of them, and even if I did, it would only make it easier on Flood. "I wouldn't know one if I tripped over him. I just met Rex."

But what I knew was that I had another conversation to have. Farley was dead. So was Rex. And Banks was missing.

Three men on a Quintile bet sheet. A trifecta. And the only person who knew that, besides me, was Michael Martin.

"No, I got somewhere else I need to be. Someone else I need to see."

The toothpick changed sides of his mouth. "Let me know if you find out something I need to know."

Chapter 10

My apartment belonged to the Buckets, late of Nashville, but these days they lived anyplace a grandchild lived. I watched the house they used to live in, collected their circulars, and lived in the garage apartment for free. It was a good deal and had been for a few years. I'd made updates to the place, and it suited me.

Unfortunately, it wasn't invisible. That would have suited me better. And because it wasn't invisible, I had a visitor.

She was sitting on the bottom step, looking a little put out. She wore a brown herringbone jacket that looked like it set her back what I made in half a year and a tan skirt that managed to show leg from her ankle to mid-thigh. Her shoes were those cork platforms that everybody was wearing, and she had an expensive-looking gold chain with a gaudy locket around her neck.

She looked better than she had the night before. Then again, today, she was conscious and that tended to do a lot for the way anyone looked. Compared to knocked out cold.

"I was beginning to think you never came home." She put out the cigarette she was smoking. "Or that this wasn't your place anymore."

"Why think that?" I put a cigarette in my mouth and waited to light it. She looked none the worse for wear, considering how she'd looked last night. "Do you always wake up in your own place?"

"Touché." She stood up and offered her hand. "You treated me better than I deserved. Thank you."

I lit the cigarette and shook her hand. "No problem." I looked up the steps. "Is that all? Or did you come to have a longer conversation?"

"You're pretty rude for a knight in shining armor."

I started up the steps and motioned for her to follow. "My armor's at the dry cleaner. Besides, it's all rusted out anyway." I opened the door when I got to the top and bowed. "If my lady will deign to enter."

"You're an idiot." She went in. "Nice place. Better than I'd expect."

"Yeah, my suite at the Hermitage got a little expensive, so I moved here."

"That's not what I meant." She gave a flustered sigh. "Can we just start over?"

I filled the kettle with water and put it on to boil. "Sure. Where do we start? At the beginning?"

She knitted her brows. "Beginning?"

"Sure. Let's start when you decided to go to Farley's place."

"He said he had something that belonged to Michael. He insisted that I come and retrieve it."

"Any idea what?" The kettle started to rumble. I spooned instant into the cups, poured in the water, and stirred.

"Something about the horse. Something that would be embarrassing to Michael."

I thought about Banks's bets. And Rex's. But Martin knew about those already. "You don't know what, though?"

"No." She took the coffee I handed her and put it down immediately. The wrinkle in her nose told me that instant coffee wasn't her cup of tea.

"And you went. Just like that."

"He made it sound urgent."

I sipped the coffee. There's something vaguely metallic about instant coffee, as if it melted some stainless off the spoon when you stirred it. "And was it?"

She brushed imaginary lint off her skirt. "I don't know."

"What's the last thing you remember?"

"We were sitting. About like this. He had fetched drinks for us both. I felt a little sleepy."

"And then?"

"And then I woke up at the club. Bertram says that you brought me there."

"Good old Bertram. He's the guy with the gold cords?"

"My underthings were. . . Well, they were not. . ."

"I know. That's how I found them. Believe me, I didn't..."

She put her hand up and interrupted me. "Yes." She reached into her jacket's pocket. "I received this."

She handed me an envelope. It was addressed to Michael Martin. Inside, I found several Polaroids. They were of her. The way I found her. With a little extra.

"In case you're wondering, this is not exactly the way I found you."

Her eyebrows rose.

"The, uh, toy you're using on yourself wasn't there when I arrived."

Her cheeks colored. "I don't remember any of that. Farley must have staged it. Made it look like I was..."

"Like you were in a stranger's house, involved in an indiscretion."

She turned red. "The pig."

"I can put this much together. Farley drugged you and put you in a compromising position. He took pictures. He planned to blackmail you."

"Planned? For God's sake, he still is. He wants ten thousand for the negatives."

"Then you don't know."

She looked blank.

"Farley was gunned down last night. In his own home, with you passed out. If I hadn't pulled you out of there, you might have been there when the meat wagon carted Farley out."

"No." She shook her head so hard the black curls shook. "He's not dead. He called me this morning and told me where to find the envelope. Then I went there to confront him, and he was gone."

"Dead men don't answer doors."

"The door wasn't locked. I went in. Uninvited, as it were."

"The last thing I saw in the living room was Farley with two bullets in him."

"He's not there now. Nobody is." She looked one way then another, as if her mind was replaying the moment.

"Blood on the floor?"

"Nothing. Not even the glasses we were drinking from." She had turned pale. "That's why I came to you. I thought you could reason with him."

"Or get the negatives."

"Well, yes."

"Did the person who called say he was Farley?"

"Not in so many words."

Now I put down my own cup. "But you thought that's who it was?"

Her voice was rising. "Who else could it be?"

"Somebody who put a couple of slugs in Farley. Someone who has the pictures he took." I leaned in close. "Was anyone else there? Or did anyone know you were going there?"

"Not a soul." She shuddered. "Jackson, I'm frightened."

I didn't say anything. But I could agree with the sentiment. She had something to be afraid of. For sure.

Chapter 11

I COULD HAVE CANCELLED the therapy. Cancelling would have been the smart play. But I'd already paid for the sessions. And if you missed without giving him forty-eight hours' notice, you paid anyway. I guessed it was a way of keeping the crazies honest. Or just a way of keeping me honest, crazy or not.

Anson was doodling on his notepad again. Apparently, nothing I was saying in the session was worth noting. But maybe he was drawing a picture of my brain.

"You say that you have a complicated relationship with these people at the club. Is it a complicated relationship with money, or is it a complicated relationship with power?"

"The problem is with money. After all, when you don't have any and everyone around you seems to have it, it means that money is the issue."

"But what does money give you?"

"It gives you the freedom to do what you want. If you have money, you don't have to work as hard. You don't have to play by everyone else's rules."

"Is that true? Do you think the rich don't have rules?"

"Sure, they do. But they make the rules. They have that privilege. They have that power. The rules that apply to the rest of us don't apply to them. That's all I'm saying."

"Can you imagine that their rules may be just as restrictive?"

"If what you are saying is that they have it bad, you're barking up the wrong tree, Anson. Any rules they impose on themselves are arbitrary. The sort of thing that you and I would find laughable."

"And yet they have those rules. What do you make of that?"

"I suppose it means there are bosses of the bosses, so to speak."

"You notice how quickly the conversation turns from money to power." His doodling stopped. "How do you exercise your own power, Jackson?"

"I suppose I say what goes for me. I won't follow their orders."

"Have you always been that way? Give me an example."

I wished I had something to doodle on. Maybe I'd bring a pad the next time. Maybe I'd turn into some kind of savant.

"I was a good child. Growing up, we all were. My brother, my sister, and I, we were not rule breakers. It would not have been tolerated by our parents.

"We had friends, of course, who were rebellious. We had plenty of opportunities to be bad. But we never were. We respected what our parents said, and we did as we were told."

"You were obedient." His voice was flat.

"I suppose so, to the naked eye. It could have appeared that we were obedient. Don't get me wrong. We were. But there was something different there. It wasn't that we were obedient so much as that we were doing what was right."

"How do you mean? Morally right? Is it a matter of morals?"

"It's not morals, if by morals you mean in the religious sense. Much more than that. It was right in the cosmos, in the scheme of things. No good comes from going against the scheme of things."

"That certainly sounds religious to me."

"It wasn't. It was a sense of not disturbing the balance. It was a matter of preserving order, a kind of elegance, if you will. To do otherwise was to invite chaos."

"What form did this orderliness take?"

He was pressing me. Doodling and pressing. "Okay, here's an example. There was this kid in my school. My age, not really a friend, more an acquaintance. He somehow came up with a pack of cigarettes and a couple of beers. We were thirteen. He wanted me to sneak off with him and drink and smoke. It's the sort of thing that all teenage boys do, right?"

He looked up from his pad. "I certainly did. Not that you care."

"No, Anson, that's good to know. It makes you a little more human."

He went back to his pad.

"But here's the thing, and maybe it makes me not so human. I said no. Even though he asked me twice and even though doing it would probably have made me more popular in the end, I said no."

"Because it would disorder the universe? That seems a leap for a teenager to make."

"No. Not the universe. Or at least not the big universe. It would have disordered my universe, the one that existed by agreement with my parents and my siblings. It would've made a change in the armor of that order. If I did that, what else would follow?"

"You make it sound like a house of cards. Not very strong, not very stable."

"Much later, I would see it in that way, but as I grew up, I saw it more as a firm foundation, covered by a house of stone. That house protected me, protected us, gave certainty. If that's the way I felt, and it was, why on earth would I tear it down? Especially over some guy, over popularity, over beer and cigarettes? It made no sense."

"When did that change? Or did it?"

"It changed in Vietnam. War doesn't care about your damn stone house. War is chaos come to life. Every day, you made up new rules, ones that would keep you alive until you made up the next set of rules."

"War is hell, isn't it? Isn't that what they say?"

"Were you ever in combat, Anson?"

He shook his head. "No."

"If you were there, you would understand, and if you weren't, you'd never understand. To say war is hell or that it is chaos is putting a word on something too complex to express.

"But it may be enough to say that combat destroyed the sense of order in my life and replaced it with something much more fluid. Some guys come back and replace it with an inflexible set of values. Could be religious, could be a set of warrior values that they have invented and taken to heart.

"Or some guys come back and replace that chaos with another form of order. A kind of order that they drink or drug their way through. It's a way of imposing order, or at least silencing the chaos, they feel in their bones."

"From what you've told me, you did that."

"Maybe." I felt myself tense then relax. "Maybe not. That's not what it felt like I was doing, but fair enough if that's the way it looks. The point is you can't just accept the chaos. You have to impose something on it."

"And once your stone house was gone?"

It was a good question. We had begun by talking about money and power and my reaction to the Harpeth Ridge set. And here we were now, a half hour later, talking about how I ordered my disordered life.

"You are good, Anson. You've tricked me again."

"I don't know what you mean. There's no trickery here. We are having a conversation, trying to understand you. At least I'm trying to understand you."

"I'm trying to understand too, Anson. But I think that's the point, isn't it?"

"That's why you pay me the big bucks, Jackson."

"Then let me go ahead and extend the metaphor. Rich people have their own stone houses. Except we don't understand how to get in and out of their houses. They know. We knock on what looks like a door because it's a door to us, but it turns out that's not the way in."

"What's the way in?"

"Who knows?"

That was the whole point. Imogene was busy keeping people out of hers, but Farley proved her wrong. Abbie probably thought she could get Daddy to buy her another house if she ruined this one. And Rex? Rex had been betting with house money, even though he had more money than he'd ever need. And he'd lost his bet down at the river.

"I think you've latched onto something that will help you make sense of the life you've been living."

"I'm not so sure about that, Anson. Seems like I'm just telling myself a story and putting myself in it."

"Isn't that what we all do, Jackson? We tell ourselves stories and hope they make sense. If they make sense to a lot of people, we call it the truth. If they stop making sense, we call them myths." He stopped doodling and looked at me. "What about your old stone house? Truth? Or myth?"

"It was truth first. After all, it worked. Then it stopped working. I guess it was a myth. But don't myths work if everyone buys the myth?

"You tell me."

"Seems like that's the way it goes. As long as everyone believes, there's no trouble. There's a shared framework. Something for everyone to get behind. But the moment that there is evidence to the contrary?"

"Like Vietnam?"

"Oh yeah, that was wholesale repudiation. But it doesn't even have to be that. It could be a single insistent chord. Or discord. My brother Thompson, for example. He was fine until he went to college. And then he stopped believing."

"What happened?"

"Nobody knows. He did a semester at college and then went west."

"You never saw him again?"

"Once. He came back home to die."

"I'm sorry." The doodling stopped momentarily "That sounds hard."

"A lot around it was hard. That's true. And since he was the third of our five to go, of all us who lived inside the stone house, it was even harder. But the point is, he had already left the house. And I don't know what changed that. But whatever it was, it was enough to bring the house down for him. The same way the war brought it down for me."

"Tell me about coming home, Jackson."

"A combat vet after he comes home is confused, lonely, and depressed. He misses his brothers, worries about them, and he misses the high, the excitement, of combat once he is out of it for good. Just about any job he gets doesn't do it for him. You can get depressed.

"After a lot of us got home, we wanted to get back. Not me, but there's more than a few. And a lot of us, knowing we would feel this way, took on more tours. A half-assed lieutenant tried that on me before I left."

He put down the pad and looked straight at me. "But you weren't having it? You knew better?"

"That was the only world they knew. The other world, this one, the one we live in now, was a scary, unreal dream world to a lot of vets."

"What made it different for you, Jackson?"

"A lot of us joined the police or fire departments to carry on the excitement."

"And yet you are not going back to the academy."

"I don't belong there. I didn't belong in Vietnam. None of us did. And now I don't belong here."

I stopped talking, and Anson was silent. We remained that way for a minute, him back to doodling on his notepad, me lost in thought. There was so much ground to cover and so few words that were adequate.

I roused myself. "Same time next week?"

He nodded. "If you're game."

"I think we've come this far. There's no harm in going further."

"I'm glad you feel that way."

I didn't know how I felt about therapy. But I felt better.

Chapter 12

WHAT LAY INSIDE FARLEY'S house, or didn't, was my immediate concern, though.

The storm from last night had left detritus all over the street, leaving it looking like an ill-tempered tree god had shaken every maple on the street and knocked everything loose that wasn't nailed down.

The brightness of the morning had subsided, and what was left was the sort of humidity you usually get in the summer. If I had to guess, I'd have bet on another storm soon.

I'd parked the Impala in a different spot on the other side of the street. This time, I could see the back porch where last night's gunman had made his getaway. I could also see the front door.

It'd have been nice if I'd thought of all that last night. But it wouldn't have solved the mystery of where Farley's body had gone.

I waited until I was sure there was no one on the premises, then I made my way to the door. In the daylight, I sauntered, as if I was someone looking for yard work or some such task. Anyone seeing me would think nothing of me.

As Imogene had said, it was unlocked, and I took my handkerchief and pushed my way in. No need to leave fingerprints that would be lifted. Wouldn't look good if I ever did go back to the academy.

I entered and saw a shadow to my left. I'm not a man who usually carries a gun, but I'd brought my Colt 1911 with me, the one that closely matched my Army sidearm. I brought it on the theory that there's nothing more dead than a man who leaves his gun at home when he's coming to a gun fight.

I tossed a vase toward the door. That would flush a shooter, I figured. That's the way most of them work. Hear a noise. Fire. Assume it's your target.

I'd seen guys in the jungle killed making that assumption.

But nobody made any assumption with the vase's noise. "You'd better come out here," I said. "I've got both exits covered. Nothing you can do to get away."

I listened. I could hear breathing. "Make it easy on yourself. Get out here."

I could almost imagine I could hear thinking. A few seconds passed. Then I saw a woman's head topped by an absurd, floppy yellow hat.

Abbie Martin.

"Don't shoot." She stepped fully through the door. She was wearing a strappy yellow sundress that somehow managed to make the hat look like an afterthought. "Oh, it's just you."

"What are you doing here?"

She gave me the canned version of the seductive look she'd tried a couple of days before. "Did you follow me?"

"Don't answer a question with a question. What do you want with Farley?"

She moved closer. "Imogene said he's dead. Didn't you know?"

"I know, all right." I had the .45 at my side. She saw it and jumped. "You killed him."

"Don't be stupid. Why would I kill him?" The girl was cute, but she wasn't a rocket scientist. "Never mind, don't answer that. Answer this: what are you doing here?"

She tried to keep the seductive look going, but it was too much effort, even for her. "I made some bets with him. If he's dead, I..."

"You don't want somebody new coming to collect?"

"That's right." She still had enough energy to scowl. "I thought maybe I could find his books. You know, where he keeps his records."

"And you don't figure that whoever killed him might be interested in those records themselves?"

Her eyes widened, and her chin dropped. "I don't know. I just figured ..."

"Yeah, you just figured you'd have a look around. Did you find anything?"

Before she could answer, a key went inside the front door lock, turned it, and the doorknob rattled. Abbie raced to the other room's door and peered around the opening. I stood there, Colt at the ready.

Inside came Willie Peele. Slowly and deliberately.

"Come in, Willie." I showed him the Colt in case he missed it.

He hadn't missed it. "Put that away. No need for it."

"There are too many people here, Willie. Too many damn unexpected people."

"Where's Farley?"

"Good question. I was just saying that to Abbie here."

Abbie came out from behind the door. Peele looked at her then looked away. He snorted. "What the hell is she doing here?"

"That's what I mean, Willie. Too many unexpected people. And the one guy you'd expect, Farley, is nowhere to be found."

"Where is he?"

I walked over to the rug, in the place where he'd been lying the night before. I pulled it up. The blood was there. "Farley's dead, Willie. That's what I think. Somebody put a couple of slugs in him last night. But they've carted the body away."

"You call the police?"

"Not me. I've got little Miss Martin here, and I'd hate for her daddy to have to explain what she's doing here. Besides, there's no body anymore."

"Then how do you know so much?"

"Funny how that works, Willie. I knew enough to be here last night. Johnny on the spot, as it happens."

"Then who killed Farley?"

"I got here just after. I heard shots, and I came in." I motioned again with the Colt. "That was unexpected. And now? More unexpected people. Makes me wonder if you had anything to do with it, Willie."

If anything, he became more unhurried and deliberate. "I don't have anything against Farley."

"You have a key to his place."

"Of course I do. I own this house."

I kept the .45 pointed down. "How does that work, Willie? You rent the house to a bookmaker? And you a horse trainer? What will people think?"

"He's a bookmaker?" Willie scratched his chin. "How about that?"

"And that's the reason he was shot, I figure. In your house. How do you feel about that, Willie?"

He scowled. "I don't get you, mister. You're big on putting yourself in the middle of my business. That's not something I'd recommend." He talked slowly, same as he moved.

"I'm on your side, Willie. I'm in the middle because of the girl here."

Abbie managed a weak smile.

"I came here to help your boss. If I'd known you were the landlord, I might have run at this a little differently."

"Well, you know now." He looked around at Farley's stuff. "Get out."

I motioned to Addie. She headed to the door, and I followed her.

There was a palpable feeling of hate in the air. Willie Peele watched me walk toward the door, slowly and deliberately. I saw Abbie to her car, and I got in the Impala. She peeled out, and I rolled forward more sedately.

I drove to the bottom of the hill and turned around, facing the house. Ten minutes later, Willie came out, got in his truck, and disappeared in the opposite direction, neither fast or chaotic but slow and steady, just as he always did everything.

I sat there for a minute just in case he came back. When he didn't, I backed the car up once more and went back to Farley's.

Chapter 13

I WENT INSIDE AND found what I wasn't looking for.

He was tall and dark and wasn't anyone's idea of handsome. His chin was too long, and his nose was too short. He wore a polyester vest over polyester pants and had paired the striped pants with a checked red and blue dress shirt. The only thing less obvious than his fashion sense was what the hell he was doing in Farley's apartment.

He stood in the doorframe of the kitchen, filling it completely except for a bit above his head. He had the attitude of someone who knew the game he wanted to play, but his smile didn't give away the game.

"Forget something?" He leaned on the doorframe. "Or just want to look around some more?"

"I've seen you down at the stables."

"That's right. Art Spatz. I do a little work here and there for Willie."

"You don't strike me as the horse type."

"You'd be surprised. Besides, horse business covers a lot of territory."

I did my own bit of leaning on my door, mirroring his attitude. "That's what I hear. Farley was in the horse business. Right?"

He grinned. Then he reached behind him and pulled out what looked like a .22 pistol. "If you're so smart, why don't you tell me all about it."

I put my hands up where he could see them. "Don't be a tough guy. There's no need."

"Maybe I ought to call the cops. Breaking in here and all."

"Sure. The phone's over there." I pointed to one of Farley's side tables. "Ask for Bobby Flood. He knows me."

He lowered the peashooter and then put it back behind him. He didn't like that I was agreeing with him, and he liked it even less that I could point to the cop I wanted him to call.

"What's your deal, Trade? What are you after?"

"I'm helping out a friend. Farley had some stuff that I need."

"Yeah? Like what?"

"Let's just say that his part of the horse business compromised my friend. Now that Farley's dead, I want it back."

He pointed to the sofa, and I sat. He took a seat on the stuffed chair that matched it. "There's nothing here. I searched."

"You don't know what I'm looking for."

"I bet I do. You want anything to do with Martin's wife or kid. That's who you're working for, right?"

"How would you know if you found what I'm looking for?"

"I'd know." He looked at me over his short nose. "There isn't anything."

"That means somebody cleaned the place out." I was thinking about Farley's body, but it made sense that that person would have taken the gambling receipts too. "Any ideas?"

"Farley had a redhead that worked for him."

"I saw her."

"Her name is LaRae Preston. She runs with a loser named Glenn Dempsey."

"Where does a guy find her?"

"They have an apartment over by the mall. You could look it up in the phonebook."

"And you figure them for Farley?"

"Hell no. LaRae is too lazy and Dempsey's too dumb. But she's got a head for opportunity, that girl does. If somebody took Farley's stuff, it'd be her."

"That why you were looking, Spatz?"

He didn't grin this time. "What I do doesn't have anything to do with you. I gave you a name. Now go find her and get out of my way."

He stood up, and I could see that he was at least as tall as he seemed when he filled the doorframe. Either the vest was a little small for him, or he had enough musculature to make the polyester bulge.

"Okay, Spatz. You've got your game and I've got mine." I stood and looked him in the eye. "Pleasure doing business with you."

"We don't have business, Trade. Remember that the next time you see me."

I walked to the door and turned to look at him. He was breathing in through his nose and out through his mouth. I heard once that's the way you meditate. If he was meditating, it was probably on the subject of how to get rid of me.

I went out and got in the Impala. It started with just the normal amount of huffing and puffing. I put it in gear and rolled down toward the west end. Nobody followed me.

I pulled into a driveway at the bottom of the hill and waited. No one came by. Not Spatz. Not anyone. I sat for a minute and then backed out into the street to continue my way toward my apartment.

No one followed. No one at all.

Chapter 14

By the time I decided what I was going to do, it was late afternoon, and the rush hour was in full swing. How Nashville gets Los Angeles-level traffic with a tenth of the population is a testament to the lack of city planning, but it sure does make little old Music City feel like a metropolis.

The apartment complex was all the way on the other side of Green Hills, out toward Hundred Oaks Mall. From the parking lot, you could see the figures of people moving past their windows without the slightest notion that they could be seen. A few walked out on their tiny balconies with a beer or a glass of iced tea, but most were consumed with the activity that comes with the end of a long day at work and too much to do when you get home. More of them should have ventured out, just for a minute. The air was cool and clean, the kind that comes after a rain in the spring. You don't get many of those days.

I had the Colt stuffed in the back of my pants. A brown barn coat covered it so that no one would think that I was anything other than someone coming by for a quick one after work. I walked up to the second-floor landing, took a left, and stood in front of apartment 211.

I pressed the button and could hear a tired buzz. People moved around inside before the door opened a crack.

"I'm looking for Farley," I said.

"Wrong place, bud." The speaker was about my height but with the kind of bald head that men his age shouldn't have. He'd made an allowance by growing the hair on the side longer than he should have. It was an unfortunate look. Someone should have let him know.

He had the chain still on the door. I got my boot toe in the opening. "I think I've got the right place. Quintile Racing. John Farley."

The man looked away from me and toward the interior of the apartment. Given that I'd contradicted him, he should have said something. But he was too busy communicating silently with someone inside.

"Like I said, nobody here by that name."

"Cut the crap." His eyes glared at me. "And make sure LaRae doesn't have something pointed at me." I pulled out the Colt. "You understand?"

He took a minute to consider if he understood, then he nodded and took the chain off the door. He stepped back into the apartment.

He had close-set black eyes that darted toward the kitchen. His face was tan, and he wore a wife-beater undershirt that showed the hairs on his back.

"Get her out here."

"Who? I don't know who you're talking about."

I yelled toward the kitchen. "Get out here, LaRae. Introduce your boyfriend to me."

He didn't like that, but he kept his mouth shut. He glanced down at the cigarette burning in his hand and stubbed it out in the ashtray. "Come on out, Sugar."

The red-haired girl from the bookie joint sashayed into the room.

"No need to shake it if you don't want to break it." I motioned with the gun. "Both of you have a seat. We have things to discuss."

"I thought you wanted an introduction." She popped her chewing gum.

"I know who Glenn Dempsey is. What I don't know is why he's here."

They both looked surprised. LaRae was the first to speak. "All right. You know Glenn and you know me. You know where I live because you're here. Big deal."

Glenn was still staring at me. The fact that I knew his name and he didn't know mine looked like it was pissing him off. The beady black eyes narrowed behind the lids. "Who is this creep?"

"I'm the guy that can make you or break you, so you'll want to keep your mouth to yourself." I leaned against the doorjamb to the kitchen, both LaRae and Dempsey in front of me. "And hand over the receipts you lifted from Farley."

LaRae jumped to her feet. "You don't know nothing."

Dempsey shot her a look, and she sat back down. "Who said anything about receipts? What kind of receipts?"

"Nice try, Glenn. I'm not trying to horn in on your action, and I'm certainly not cleaning up the Dixie Mafia's territory. If they don't mind, it don't matter."

He chewed his lip over that and looked away from me.

"But I can get a little antsy over the blackmail business. Running a sports book is one thing. Bleeding somebody over dirty pictures is a whole different deal."

"Who says I'm blackmailing anybody?"

"I do. Farley was. Now you took over the business."

He cleared his throat roughly.

"I know you took the business. The question is whether you killed him to get the business."

"Like hell." Dempsey's eyes were on the Colt. If we'd been a little closer, I had no doubt we'd be wrestling for it. "How do you figure it?"

"Here's the way I think it went. You showed up at Farley's. Maybe you thought he was alone. Maybe you just didn't care. But it turned out that he was working another little blackmail, and you lucked out. You got those pix, and you got all Farley's books. Trouble is, you had to put a couple of slugs in him in the process."

Dempsey's mouth formed a tight grin. "You think you've got me made for this, then?"

"Doesn't matter if you give me what I want."

LaRae was sitting on the edge of the couch cushion.

Dempsey ran his tongue along his teeth under his lips. "You must think I'm stupid."

"Not really. At least not more than any garden-variety gambler. Just give me the pictures and the receipts, and we'll call it even."

"I don't know what you're talking about."

"Don't be obtuse, Glenn. I'm giving you a chance to get out from under this, and you're giving me lip. You called Imogene Martin and faked that you were Farley this morning. You've got gambling receipts on Rex Cameron, Abbie Martin, and the jockey, Banks. You have all that either because you killed Farley, or you know who did."

He closed his eyes. "I don't suppose you'd come up with a little something for my trouble?"

"Not a chance, Glenn. I'm already doing you a huge favor not saying what I know."

He seemed to think about his situation. LaRae wasn't talking. She was off the edge of the cushion and curled up now like a tissue that'd been tossed away. "What if I told you I didn't do it?"

"You'll need a better story than the one I've got."

"Try this on for size, then. You're right. I've got the books and the pictures. I didn't know about the Cameron kid and the rest of the bets, but I saw the camera, and I had the film developed. It didn't take a genius to figure out what was going on there."

"So you put the pinch on Mrs. Martin."

"Sure. You might have too."

"Not a chance, man."

"Whatever you say. You might if you were broke like me. Anyway, I came in after you. I saw you haul her ass into the Mustang and drive away."

"You took Farley's body?"

"I don't know anything about that. He was lying on the floor, deader than a doornail, when I left."

"And you were there, waiting, before I went in." I still had the gun in my hand. I was sure I wasn't going to need it now. Glenn Dempsey wasn't the killer. "Who went in, Glenn? Who put two in Farley?"

He looked at LaRae. She was still tissue paper. "It was the Cameron kid. He went in, I heard shots, then he came out and peeled away in a little blue sportscar."

"And you just sat tight."

"Well, you were in there before I could get out of the car. I waited for you, then I went in."

"It's a weak story, Glenn. But it could work."

"It's the truth."

"Fine. Go get the pictures and the receipts, and we'll call it even."

"You bastard."

"It's either that or I let the Dixie Mafia know you're taking over Farley's business. I had a talk with them. They're already not amused."

He looked again at LaRae. There was no help there for him. He got his suit jacket and put a hand in its breast pocket. "Here."

I took the envelope from him.

"Pictures are in that. The Martin kid's receipts too. If you want to wait, I'll go find the others. Cameron's and Banks's, you said?"

I let him go to the bedroom, but I kept my eyes on him as I stood in the door between him and LaRae. He found the receipts and handed them to me.

"Are we square now?"

I put the receipts in the envelope with the pictures and slipped it into my back pocket. "We're square, Glenn. And just for the record, I believe you about not killing Farley. I never really made you for it, anyway."

"Thanks. I think."

"You're an opportunist, Glenn. Not a killer. But the people on the other side of this deal are killers. If I were you, I'd take LaRae and get out of Nashville."

"You think it's that dangerous for us?" He was working himself into a nasty little testosterone knot, the kind that might make him take on an impossible fight.

"I think it's less dangerous somewhere else." And if he knew what was good for him, he'd find that place sooner rather than later.

Chapter 15

The phone rang its insistent, unyielding ring. I ignored it and then gave up.

"Whoever you are, this better be good."

The silence on the other end lasted ten seconds. I was about to hang up when I heard an almost hyperactive whisper. "Trade? Is that you?"

Who the hell else would it be? That's what I wanted to say. "Yes, it's me, but your meter is running. Who is this?"

Her whisper was so loud I didn't know why she was bothering. "It's LaRae Preston."

"I already told you. You two clowns are off the hook."

"It's not that." Her whisper had a good bit of throat put into it. "I just got hold of some information you'll want."

"Since when are you helping me, LaRae?"

"Since you did us a solid. You want the information or not?"

"I'm game. Shoot."

"That horse? Fool's Trade?"

"Yeah?"

"It's dead. Keeled over in its stall sometime tonight."

That was certainly one way to get out from under bets you didn't want to honor. "Who says?"

"Never mind that." The whisper was all but a regular voice now, like she had gotten tired of being loud enough to be quiet and was now just going to be quiet in her loud voice. "I figured you'd want to know. It might do you some good."

There were a lot of things I might like to know. Where was Farley's body? Where was Banks? How was Imogene stupid enough to go to Farley's place? Why did Abbie Martin even think about betting on horses with a bookie?

Knowing a horse was dead? Why did I want to know that? "How did it die?"

"How the hell should I know?" Her voice had given up all pretense of whispering. "If you don't care, then forget about it. I shouldn't have called."

"Don't be mad, LaRae. I just don't get it. Was the horse sick?"

"Like I said, I don't know. Somebody told me. I thought you might want to know."

And she hung up the phone. The click in my ear wasn't a whisper either.

I rubbed my ear and dialed up Martin.

"He's not here," Imogene said. "He's down at the stable."

"When did he find out?"

"An hour ago. He dragged his sorry ass out of bed and got dressed, still smelling like last night's bottle."

I could imagine. "Pretty upset, I guess."

"I wouldn't call it upset, really. More like he had business to attend to. Autopilot, you know."

I wouldn't know. If I had a horse worth a couple of million dollars and it croaked, I would probably be down there trying to breathe life back into it with a little mouth-to-mouth.

When I got there, there was a small group. Willie Peele. A couple of the grooms. No sign of Martin.

I backed Willie toward the stool in the corner of the stall. He sat somewhat reluctantly, but he sat nevertheless. "Did you find him this way?"

"No. One of the boys found him as he made rounds for the last feed of the night. He came running. I was in the small barn with one of my other horses. I have no idea what happened. He seemed fine."

"You were in here just a little before?"

"Probably about an hour, hour and a half. Once we put the horses in for the night, there's no reason for me to be here. Actually, except for last feed, there's no reason anyone would be here."

"So you are likely the last to see him alive?"

"I would guess so. I'm usually the last one out of every barn except for the boys."

He sighed, and I could see the pent-up tension begin to exit his body. "The horse had a hard time these last two years. Started out as a really promising flat racer before the foreleg problem showed up. Then had a good run as a jumper. He had to take a year off then had a good year last year."

"There's nothing to suggest that the horse had anything physically wrong with it?"

"Not at all. But these animals are finely tuned machines. Sometimes, it's like one small thing goes wrong, and the system, so well balanced, just shuts down in a cascade of body failures. I've seen it before. It's sad, but it's a part of the business."

"So you don't think ..."

"I don't think what? That there's something fishy here? I'd be shocked, really surprised. This just happens. But we'll see. The horse is insured, so there will be a necropsy. That's required by the policy, but

I would be surprised if the verdict came back as anything but colic, cause unknown. That's kind of the catchall."

"Who does the necropsy?"

"The doc at UT vet school might come up and do it, but we have a few people in Nashville that seem to be okay by the insurance companies. We'll just have to see. It's up to them."

"In the meantime?"

"In the meantime, Bud Simms will come and make a preliminary assessment. He's our large-animal vet. We called him as soon as we could."

Willie proved correct. In about ten minutes, a big, broad-shouldered guy about forty years old stood in the stall door. He wore rubber Wellingtons and looked for the world like what you would envision if you were envisioning a large-animal vet. Strong through the thighs and torso, with rope-like forearms, the sort of guy who could wrestle a foal out of the birth canal with finesse and still be strong enough to hold down the mare with the other hand. He looked like a guy you wouldn't want to mess with, except for the friendly face and mouth set in a near-perpetual smile. He paired that smile now with eyes that communicated sadness. They were drawn down. "Hey, Willie. What have we got here?"

"He was fine last night."

"Well, it's clear that there'll have to be a postmortem," he said, "but I can have a look and see if anything jumps out at me."

He nodded once at me, never asking who I was or what I was doing there. He didn't know me, but he knew the horse and he knew the trainer, and that was all he really needed to know to do his job.

He began by putting on gloves that covered up to near his elbow. He checked the horse's eyes, looked in his mouth, smelled, and took his time working his way around the horse's body. He palpated a couple of times and made a sort of mental note, it seemed, to himself. He rolled the horse so that he could get access to his midsection and palpated again. Then he took one hand and reached inside the horse from behind, apparently looking or feeling for something.

"What's he doing?" I asked Willie.

"Probably checking to see if he's got torsion in his bowels. It's the sort of thing that happens to horses and it kills them, right quick. Problem is, there's usually not a lot of advance notice."

The vet overheard our conversation, and as he pulled his arm out of the horse and snapped off the gloves, he said, "That's right. But I don't feel any torsion."

"Got any idea, Doc?" Willie said it, but not with much feeling. He seemed to have moved on from the death of the horse and had other things on his mind.

"No idea. It will take a full postmortem to tell what's going on here. I don't want to guess." He stubbed the toe of his boot at the horse's left front leg. "That leg been doing okay lately?"

Willie shifted on the stool. "You know how these things go. Some days, everything's roses, and some days, it seems like it's all thorns. Nothing to keep them going over fences, mind you, especially if we spend our time making sure that he doesn't get overworked."

"Well, if there's nothing else, Willie, I'll get along. Nighttime is time for me to be close to the house."

I followed the vet out of the barn. "You get a lot of nighttime emergency calls, Doc?"

"Yes, sir. More than I like, more than you'd expect. I don't believe I caught your name." He shook a cigarette out of a pack that had magically appeared.

Before he could light it, I produced my Zippo and struck a flame.

"Much obliged."

I took one of my own and lit it. "Name's Jackson Trade. What do you really think about what you saw in there?"

"Don't have the slightest idea. Horses are delicate creatures. And they're not smart enough to tell us when they're in distress."

"This happens a lot?"

"Not a lot. These chasers probably have the best life of any thoroughbred. By the time they get too old to steeplechase, they're coming right into the right age to be a show jumper. And if they're not going to be a show jumper, well, there's all sorts of things they can do. Bring along the next generation, if you know what I mean." He grinned. "They generally have an easy life."

He took a draw and enjoyed the exhale. "Eight or ten times a year, somebody climbed on his back, and he would run three or four miles, jumping over fences and hedges. It's all over in about twelve minutes, front to back." He finished the butt and stubbed it out on the ground. "Hell, if I only had to work eight or ten times a year for twelve minutes each, and in return got to play outside all day and eat all I wanted? Then chase the ladies? I think I'd take that deal. Wouldn't you, Trade?"

"Yeah." It did seem like a sweet deal. And not one that would have put enough pressure on Fool's Trade's body that he'd die.

But then, horses are delicate creatures. Not like humans at all.

Chapter 16

GETTING INVITED TO THE inquest had been easy enough. Bud Simms had asked to be included, which was a courtesy to the attending vet, and he had asked me to come with him. Michael Martin and Willie gave me a serious case of side-eye, but they said nothing.

The report took place in the boardroom at the country club. The insurance company sent a guy in a suit, and he started the meeting but soon handed over the proceedings to a man he introduced as Dr. Paul Kraposky.

As much as the suit looked like a corporate shill, Kraposky looked like a mad scientist. Even though he'd found a suit to wear, it didn't fit, and the tie he chose was badly tied and mismatched to the suit. His hair had a mind of its own and had resisted any attempt, if there had been any attempt, to make it behave. His mustache was bushy and appeared to still retain something of breakfast. A tiny bit of scrambled egg, if I saw correctly.

His voice was nasal and betrayed a Chicago point of origin, sort of like the obnoxious Bears fan who once lived next door to me. The accent was unmistakable, especially if the Bears were down a couple of touchdowns. Once he began to speak as a scientist, however, the accent receded, and the room fell silent.

"Sudden death, which I will designate as SD henceforth, associated with exercise in racehorses, is an infrequent event. But when it occurs, it poses a serious risk to jockeys and horses alike. Usually more to the horse, to be honest, but humans have a tendency to value themselves as well." He looked up. Not to see if we were laughing. He wasn't joking.

"I am using the term 'exercise-associated sudden death,' to which I will refer in future as EASD. In particular, I use it to refer to cases of SD that occur during exercise or within one hour postexercise. The term 'sudden cardiac death' I'll refer to as SCD, and I'll use that to refer to those cases of SD or EASD in which there is no apparent reason or cause of death during the postmortem examination and histologic examination of extracardiac tissues."

I gave my own side-eye to Simms. He shook his head. "I'll translate later."

"These cases of SCD are then 'necropsy-negative,' as there are no lesions to explain the cause of death. Incidentally, in my own published studies, I have recorded multiple postmortem findings in cases of SD or EASD in equine populations. Recorded causes of SD or EASD in these studies have ranged from exercise-induced pulmonary hemorrhage to pulmonary edema and hemorrhage to massive thoracic and/or abdominal bleedings, cardiac tamponade as a result of aortic rupture, skull or cervical neck fractures, myocardial fibrosis, and arteriosclerosis. Sad to say, these studies have various autopsy and histologic sampling methods, and their results and interpretations of the findings are inconsistent."

Now, Martin and Willie were glazing over. "Can you get to the point, Doc?" Willie was terse, but his annoyance was clear.

Undeterred, Kraposky went on as if Willie hadn't spoken. "As a result, any valid conclusions about the underlying events that lead to EASD and SCD are difficult to attain, and therefore, the pathogenesis and possible cause or causes of EASD and SCD in horses such as these remain largely unclear.

"In fact, in many cases of equine EASD, the cause is not apparent during autopsy, and it is then generally presumed to be acute cardiac, cardiovascular, or cardiorespiratory failure. For that reason, the examination of the cardiovascular system is warranted. And that is what I did." He looked up to see if we were attending correctly. Satisfied, he continued.

"The equine SD autopsy protocol I performed was extensive. I used a variety of histological screens.

"This is what I looked for, based on my experience. Microscopic heart lesion. These lesions include inflammation of the myocardium, epicardium, endocardium, and valves, fibrosis, acute myocardial degeneration and necrosis, myocardial dropout, as well as miscellaneous lesions. However, it is vital to emphasize that the interpretation of the clinical significance of these lesions is challenging, given that many horses without a history of SD or EASD, ones that are euthanized because of catastrophic musculoskeletal injuries, will have similar lesions.

I looked around the table. Everyone except Simms and the insurance suit had the same look on his face that I had.

Which translated to two simple questions: What did he just say? And what did it mean?

Simms had picked up on the confusion. "I think what he means, if you'll permit me, Doc, is that the postmortem doesn't demonstrate conclusively what killed Fool's Trade. Is that the gist of it?"

"That's right. The absence of lesions would indicate EASC. But the history of the horse and the context of his death, with no exercise in its immediate past, rule that out. However, with SCD, there would be lesions, almost certainly. There always are at least microscopic lesions. The horse had none of those, however. Therefore, we cannot conclusively state a cause of death."

"Colic." Willie had raised himself to a commanding position, standing like a schoolboy who'd been called on. "Lots of times, we don't know what kills them. Vet certifies it as 'colic, cause unknown.'"

"Except in this case, Willie, we know it wasn't colic." Willie had resumed his seat and was looking down at the table. Simms continued, "I knew it wasn't colic that night. And the lab boys confirmed it, right, Doc?"

Kraposky nodded. "We looked specifically. As we did for any cause of death. This was a most thorough examination."

Even though I had several questions, I kept my mouth shut. Soon enough, I'd have a conversation with Simms. Maybe he could give me the answers I needed.

***

He took the cigarette I offered, and we smoked in silence for a few minutes. "Kraposky is a specimen," I said. "Almost a stereotype."

"Maybe. But he's good. One of the best equine pathologists in the country."

"What do they do, exactly? I could barely get through his gobbeldy-gook."

"The procedure is pretty straightforward. Before any animal is examined, he takes a history. I gave that to him.

"Then Kraposky dissected the horse to get a clear look at every part of its body. He's looking for abnormalities. If he sees lesions, they're recorded and sampled for further testing.

"He takes a lot of tissue samples, even if they look okay. He looks at some, but he probably sends others out to other labs."

"Sounds thorough," I said. I imagined that Kraposky would be totally into it. Seemed like it would be his sort of thing.

"It should be. Horses like this are worth thousands. Some, like Fool's Trade, are heavily insured. You have to know why the horse died."

"It's a big deal that Kraposky says it's inconclusive?"

"It means there will be a fight about it."

"In court?"

"If it gets that far. They may settle."

"That happens most of the time, eh?" I could imagine it could be easier than getting the lawyers involved. Cheaper too.

"It happens sometimes. But I don't think so in this case."

"Why's that?"

"Something about the way the insurance guy set his jaw. And there's something else."

"Martin doesn't like to lose either?"

"I bet Martin doesn't like to lose. But that isn't it. There's always a cause of death. There's always a reason. If an ace like Kraposky says the cause is inconclusive? It's fishy. Too damn fishy."

"You got a theory, Simms?"

"Not the first hint of one. But I don't like it."

Chapter 17

I HAD SAID TO Simms that he seemed knowledgeable about the horses. "If you want to talk to someone who really knows, meet me at Bill's Gym tomorrow morning at six. I'll introduce you to somebody who really knows horses."

I knew Bill's Gym. It was a real lifting gym, not the sort I'd spent time in as an undergrad, the sort that had Universal machines and some Nautilus equipment. Sure, there were free weights and dumbbells around, and other fitness equipment, but most people contented themselves with doing circuits around the Universal or the Nautilus.

Bill's was a different animal entirely. One wall was squat racks. The opposite wall had benches with racks, although the bench could be removed, turning it into a competition squat rack. In the middle was plenty of room for deadlifting. It was barely six o'clock when I arrived, and already, there were a half-dozen men. Most of them were quite large, setting up to do their day's work. I got the impression from the looks on their faces that they had indeed come to work, not to gab and lift a little.

I spotted Simms in the corner. He was pulling on knee sleeves. His face broadened as if he might laugh. "Well, Trade, at least you know how to dress when you come to a gym."

I had on a T-shirt that had a rust stain on the neckline, and a pair of running shorts. "What? A gym is a gym, right?"

"The gym is most surely not your usual gym, my friend. And the first thing I usually have to tell someone is just come barefoot if you're going to wear your fancy Nike waffle trainers. But you, for whatever reason, picked the exact right shoes."

I looked down. I wore an old pair of red Chuck Taylor high-tops that I'd had since my senior year of high school, more than ten years ago. They were ratty, but they were what I had in terms of athletic shoes. "These?"

"Exactly. They're flat and don't cushion your foot too much. Perfect for deadlifts, not bad for squats. Which is what I'm doing today. If you're working out with me, it's what you're doing too."

He tossed me a pair of knee sleeves. "Put these on after we warm up, and you'll be set."

We went through a fairly extensive warmup. At least it was more than I normally would have done. I think my idea would have been about fifteen jumping jacks, some toe touches, and call it good. Simms was doing nothing of the sort. We went through a whole series of shoulder-loosening exercises then some stretches for the front part and then the back part of the leg. All this culminated in our sitting in a pronounced squat position for about five minutes. All the while, he was telling me what to feel and where to stretch. By the time we were done, I felt like I'd had a workout already. But I had to admit I felt pretty loose. And my ankle felt almost limber.

"Let's head for the rack up front. That's where James Lee will be.

"The guy you want me to talk to?"

"The one and only. Guy knows more about steeplechase than any-body in middle Tennessee."

"More than Willie Peele?"

"Listen, James Lee taught Willie everything he knows, which is half of what James Lee knows because he doesn't have time to tell everything he knows."

We approached a squat rack, where a short, burly man with a bald head and a black beard was settling in under the bar. He looked to be about five foot five and seemed like he could easily be that wide too. His broad shoulders settled into the bar. He brought his hands in, causing his shoulders to form a ledge onto which he settled the bar. It looked to be loaded with about three hundred pounds. Since I made him at about one hundred fifty pounds, that would mean the bar was twice his weight.

"Watch this," said Simms. "This is a warmup set."

James Lee unracked the bar and took two baby steps back, one with each foot. He settled, took a deep breath, and tensed. Then he began to descend so that his butt almost touched the floor. He held that for just an instant. Then he powered up, seeming not to notice that he had weight on his back. He repeated the same routine four more times: breathe, brace, then squat and rise. When he racked the weights, he turned around relatively quickly and, upon seeing Simms, walked up and shook his hand. "Bud, my buddy. How's life in the veterinarian business?"

"Looking good, James Lee. And this is a rookie who's come to strain your brain. Jackson, meet James Lee."

"If you're a friend of Bud here, you and I will get along fine." He looked me up and down as we shook hands. "Not a lifter, but athletic enough. That long frame will be a bit of problem for the deadlift.

And squats might be a challenge. Just because those legs are long. But welcome! Welcome to Bill's. Who's got next?"

Simms said he would. "And Jackson, take notes."

Simms was about my size, a little shorter, a little wider. I figured to watch the weight he was moving and perhaps take it down by twenty percent. When I saw him leave the three hundred on the bar, I recalculated. Sims was nowhere near as fluid as James Lee, but he was just as effective in moving the bar up and down. He did his five and then looked at me as I pulled on the knee sleeves. "Where do you want to start, Jackson? We can warm up with one forty-five and see how you go."

I thought that might be shooting low, but I said nothing. Better to look strong and have more weight than to look bad.

"What you do is, get settled in there, and make a little ledge with your traps."

"Like this?" I did the best I could.

"Not exactly. But don't worry about it. Just be comfortable, unrack, and step back."

I did as I was told. I took a deep breath and held it.

"Now squat."

I descended, waited, and then came up.

"Okay, hold up." James Lee came around to the side of the squat rack. "Watch me," he said. "This is a squat movement," and he went down almost as low as our warm-up squats that we held for minutes. "But this is what you did." This time, he descended so that his legs were bent at about a forty-five-degree angle. "That's a half squat. There may be uses for that, but I can't think of any. You've got to get low."

He slid a wooden box behind me. "That should be about the right height. When you squat, make sure your butt touches the box."

It was a gentle enough instruction, but I felt embarrassed. I thought I had done a pretty good squat. Clearly, I hadn't done squat. So to speak.

Next time, I did the same. Unracked, stepped back, took a breath, and tensed. This time, I went down slowly, waiting to feel the box. At an impossibly low point. I finally felt it.

"There you go," said James Lee. "Now explode up."

I wanted to explode. My mind told my legs to explode. But what happened was that I went up as slowly as I had descended. And my ankle barked.

"Great rep," said James Lee. "Four more."

The four repetitions following were just as slow, and by the fifth, my legs felt like they were shaky. I racked the bar with its hundred and forty-five pounds on it. "That was hard."

"You're just not used to it," said Simms. "You got a good build, and you're not in bad shape for a guy that doesn't work out. We get you in here three days a week, maybe with a couple extra days of cardio work, and you will be a beast."

I wasn't sure I wanted to be a beast. But I had to admit that once the shakiness passed, I felt strong.

They took it easy on me. They continue to work up in weight until both were doing pretty solid single reps at four hundred fifty pounds. At that weight, I thought I could see the bar bend just a little. I mentioned it to Simms.

He laughed. "That's not a bend. Wait until you see James Lee pull seven hundred off the floor. That," he said, with emphasis, "is a bar that bends."

"Can you deadlift seven hundred pounds too?"

"Hell no. But James Lee is built for the deadlift. Short legs, long arms, powerful posterior chain."

My part of the workout was nowhere near as impressive, and there was no bending of the bar going on at all. But they did work me up to a single rep at a hundred seventy-five pounds, and I felt excited when James Lee clapped me on the back and said, "Great depth on that last one. Last rep, best rep, brother."

It should have been great depth. I was pretty sure my butt hit my heels. But that could have just been my imagination.

The workout done, we sat on benches in the locker room. Both Simms and James Lee had bottles they had pulled from their gym bags. "Electrolytes, some supplements," said James Lee to my inquisitive look.

It occurred to me to ask if supplements meant steroids. They had been in the news. But I decided to let it go.

"You want to know something about horses." James Lee had the steady, unwavering look of someone who was accustomed to having straight conversations.

"Steeplechase. Nashville Sweepstakes in particular."

"James Lee's your boy," said Simms.

"He may oversell what I know because I ran in those circles for a long time."

I looked at him. He was muscular and athletic and, except for the bald head, looked reasonably young.

"Yeah, I'm older than I look. All this lifting keeps me looking young. That and coloring my beard." He winked. "You might get my joints to tell a different story. They take a lot of the stress. But good form, good diet, and virtue go a long way."

"Did you pick up virtue working the steeplechase?"

He drank from his bottle. "Virtue is nothing more than discipline. How much do you know about the noble sport?"

"Just what I've been told lately. And what I've observed."

"He's been hanging out over by the country club paddocks," said Simms.

"Then you were around when the horse was found dead."

"You already heard about that?" But then I guessed a horse guy had connections. "I was raised on the farm, and I've seen dead animals before. I've never seen one that was worth that much money be dead before."

"Farm boy, eh? Then you do not know the first thing about the noble sport. Or rather, you see as through a glass darkly."

That sounded familiar. "One of the epistles, right? 'But then face to face?' About how we will only know the truth once we get to heaven?"

"A religious scholar, Simms. You've brought me Erasmus."

I may have blushed; my cheeks felt a little warm.

"But no, I was thinking of the poem by Arthur Hugh Clough, which is based on the verse in Corinthians:

Rules baffle instincts—instincts rules, Wise men are bad—and good are fools, Facts evil—wishes vain appear, We cannot go, why are we here?

"You see, the whole facade of steeplechase, from the very beginning, is that it was friendly. Oh, sure, there were side wagers between riders, and no doubt spectators got into the sport by wagering. But there was always a forced good humor about it. These were people who loved horses, and their love for the animals kept them from doing anything that would harm the animals. But they likely always did stupid things in the name of wisdom or goodness." He took a long sip of his drink. "Both illusions, by the way."

"Is a professional jockey a stupid thing?"

"Not so much. Steeplechase has been professionalized in Europe for some time now. And the whole scene has a carnival atmosphere. Hell, even here in Nashville. Lately, it's taking on the flavor of a sport that people other than the upper crust can enjoy. If you've ever seen the hill overlooking the steeple track, filled with people bearing coolers full of beer and screaming just like it was the Kentucky Derby infield, you'd know that it's no longer just the country club and the hunt club set. It's grown its own proletariat wing."

He was a poetry-quoting weightlifter who used words like "proletariat." I looked at him in amazement. He smacked my knee. It hurt a little.

"I have a feeling there's more to you, Jackson, than you let on. You might know some big words too. And more importantly, you might well use them correctly. We'll be here Wednesday at six. Why don't you come back? We'll do some Romanian deadlifts and then get to the main event."

"Which is?" I wasn't sure I wanted to know.

"Bench press." He tapped my chest. "I suspect you will do well. And we'll talk some more about horses."

"And about wise men and fools?"

"Of course. Can't talk about horses without that." He walked away, peeling clothes as he went.

"That's our James Lee," Simms said. "Not another guy like him in Tennessee. Three-time national champ in his age group and weight class. Holds every record in Tennessee worth having."

"But he got out of the horse game. What does he do now?"

"I don't ask him much. With James Lee, there's no telling." I thought I saw the very trace of a twinkle in his eye. "They say, the less you know about some things, the better."

"What's James Lee's full name, Simms?"

"Why?"

"If he's who I think he is, he could answer a lot more questions that I've got."

"Penny."

"James Lee Penny?"

"I've heard him called that. But not in here. Here, he's just James Lee."

James Lee was a national champ. James Lee Penny? He was a whole different kettle of fish.

Chapter 18

Captain Eustace Montagne had moved up quickly in the Metro PD not because he was black, as the white officers liked to complain, but because he was smart and worked hard. He was also a mean son of a bitch and took no prisoners, so to speak. Bobby Flood both hated him and respected him.

Montagne studied me while he sat at his desk. He held a finger to the side of his mouth and almost used it to turn his face, as if looking at me with the other eye would solve something for him. I'd explained how I'd been at the police academy and that I took on a little private work here and there.

"If you're academy, why am I looking at a business card that doesn't say that?" He narrowed the eye closest to me. "And in either case, why the hell do I want to talk to you?"

"I am chasing down a matter for Michael Martin. You know him?"

"What kind of matter?"

"It's not anything that Metro would be concerned with. It's personal," I lied. Metro might very well be interested in gambling and blackmail, but the purpose in hiring me was to keep them from getting interested. "But I thought maybe there was something I could do for you, and then you might be able to help me."

"We're back to you. Help you with what?"

"You didn't answer about Martin. I expect you do know him. Rich guy. Has connections downtown. District Attorney's office. Chief's office. He knows everybody."

"Maybe I heard of him. Still doesn't make me understand who you are and what you're doing here." He leaned back, his hands making a steeple under his chin, as if he had decided what he thought of me after all. "Well?"

"I don't want to waste your time, Captain." I stood up. "Bobby Flood thought you might like to know what I know."

I was motionless. He was too. Still staring at me.

"Flood?" He reached for the phone on his desk, punched in three digits, and waited. "Bobby? Eustace Montagne here. Guy named Trade claims he knows you." He listened. I could hear the muffled squawk of a voice on the other end. "Says he was in the academy." He looked at me. "Yeah, I guess that makes sense."

Eustace Montagne pointed at the chair in front of me. "Sit."

I did.

"Talk. Don't leave things out." He shifted, crossing his legs. "Flood says you do that sometimes."

"Flood doesn't appreciate how I tell the story. That's all."

"Might be. Make me appreciate it."

"Okay, it goes like this. Michael Martin is stinking rich. He's got a daughter who is trouble and a second wife who should know better but doesn't."

"Money can't get you everything."

"You got that right. Anyway, he hires me to sort out some trouble the ladies got into. I've done that."

"Good for you. Sounds like you earned your pay, then."

"Except there's some other stuff that doesn't make sense."

"If you're waiting for life to make sense, you'll be waiting a while. Trust me. The things that are perfectly normal in Nashville don't make sense half the time."

"Like Banks. The missing jockey."

"And so the shoe finally drops." He uncrossed his legs and rolled his chair closer to the desk. He put his elbows on the surface and put his hands together. They were massive hands. One inside the other, they looked like a sledgehammer. "You want to know what I know about Banks."

"If you can."

"If I can." He snorted. "You spent enough time at the academy to know that I'm not telling you shit."

"That's half the equation, Captain. It's what I could tell you that might make the exchange attractive."

"You know Banks?"

"Never laid eyes on him. English guy. Somebody said he didn't think his stuff stank."

"Sounds like a real peach."

"Mrs. Martin sized him up. My guess is that she did more than that."

"That a fact?" For a guy who'd made his career move fast, Montagne wasn't moving his body at all. His mind, though? Different story. "Mr. Martin tell you that? He could have let us know."

"That's not where I got it, Captain. But there's more."

Montagne didn't look more interested. That was his gift, I guess, when interrogating a suspect. But I detected something in the way he cleared his throat before he stuck a menthol in his mouth. "I'm listening."

"Banks was going to ride Fool's Trade in the Sweepstakes. The horse was trained by Willie Peele. Peele didn't have any use for Banks."

Montagne looked away, maybe trying to decide if he wanted to give me anything or maybe just because I bored the hell out of him. "I know Peele."

"You know him because he was a bookie's landlord, and the bookie is dead."

His head snapped back, and he focused on me. "Flood said you always know more than anybody thinks." And he smiled. Sort of. Or maybe he just gritted his teeth and decided to share. "You're telling the story, Trade. Keep going."

"I'm giving you what I got. Banks was betting against the horse, using Farley as a bookie. Farley's landlord is Peele, who hates Banks. Farley gets himself killed."

"Like you said, doesn't make sense."

"You said that, Captain. But here's one more nugget. It either makes no sense or it makes complete sense."

"Give it."

"The horse is dead now."

His mouth opened, and he started to say something. Then he stopped and shut his mouth. But laugh lines that I'd never noticed crinkled around his eyes, and his face relaxed. "All right, Trade. I didn't know about the horse. I don't think it makes finding Banks any easier, but it's a strange little detail in a strange missing-person case."

"Is it worth helping me out?"

"I thought you'd finished your job for Martin."

"Not quite. The horse complicates it."

"If you've been paid, what's your interest?"

"I think somebody killed the horse. I don't know how. And I don't know why. But Banks might." Now it was me who leaned up on the desk. "I've given you what I know, Captain. Is there anything you can give me?"

Eustace Montagne looked over my head, calculating all the reasons he could tell me to pound sand. He looked down, met my eyes. "You're a strange one, Trade. But I guess if you're working for Martin and Banks is his employee, it might help us to help you."

"Exactly what I was thinking."

"Funny you should say that Banks and the missus might have had a fling. Because that's not what we heard at all."

"Well, like I said, nobody exactly told me that."

"They might not have. Because we don't think Banks is missing at all. We think he ran off with a woman." He looked pleased with himself.

"Wouldn't be the first time, I guess. Any idea who the woman is?"

"Yeah. Funny thing there. Woman named Vera. Vera Peele."

"I didn't know Willie had a daughter."

"He doesn't. Vera is his wife."

Chapter 19

I should have gone to see Martin, but I didn't want to see him. Instead, I went to my apartment and enjoyed the new back door I'd put in on the west side, the side that before had nothing but wall. I enjoyed the window I'd put in there too. I sat in my favorite easy chair, turned toward the new door and the new window, and sipped on a beer until both the can and the beer inside were warm.

I had almost convinced myself to take a nap when the phone rang.

It was Imogene, and she said that Martin wasn't feeling all that well. The horse dying. The bets. Farley being killed. It was enough to get a man down, even if he wasn't mainlining bourbon. I could sympathize. Really, I could.

"He wants to know if you're done." Her voice had a hint of tension to it.

"With the part he was paying me for? Sure. That's a wrap." I recognized a little tension in my own voice. "Nobody will know about the bets, and Farley's business associates aren't in any position to advance the interests." I let a beat slip in between sentences. "Did he ever find out about the pictures?"

"No." She had her own beats to let sit between thoughts. "I never told him about those. But you retrieved them too?"

"Yeah, I have them. And unless you're in the mood to collect that kind of thing, I think it's best that I destroy them."

"Yes, do that." Another of her infernal beats. Talking to her on the phone was like waiting for the next bus at the bus stop. "You're sure there aren't any more?"

I didn't think LaRae and her buddy had the nerve to hold out on me. "I'm sure."

That was that. We exchanged short sentences and silences for another minute or two and said goodbye. She assured me that Martin would probably call me, and I could drop off the betting receipts. She implied that he'd pay a bonus.

As far as I could tell, the bonus was the one he'd got that he didn't know about: keeping his wife's naked pictures out of the wrong hands.

Around five, I finally gave up staring out the window without a drink in my hand, and I poured a couple of fingers of bourbon in my water glass. The first sip burned my lips, but after that, the taste was smooth enough, at least as smooth as a cheap bourbon gets.

I was looking out the window, but I was really taking the tally in my mind. Parker Street hired me to find a jockey, but the jockey wasn't found. He maybe was having a fling with the owner's wife, but he seemed to have run away with the trainer's wife. I didn't know what Vera Peele looked like, and she was probably an easier partner than Imogene Martin, but Martin was where the money was. So keep the box open next to Banks's name. I hadn't found him. Metro hadn't found him either.

But it might not be that big a deal. He didn't have a horse to ride anyway since Fool's Trade had punched his ticket to the pasture in the sky. Bud Simms thought it was a little dodgy, and he wasn't the only one since I agreed, but there was nothing to say if the expert horse doc was satisfied. And the insurance company too.

Maybe Banks could come back and ride Rex's horse, since dead men don't ride. But maybe that filly would be just as happy grazing and cantering around.

One thing for sure. Nobody would be putting any bets on any of that with Farley now. And LaRae wasn't covering any of the action. And James Lee Penny, who oversaw all the action in town, wouldn't have to worry about Farley horning in on his organization's business.

If he ever was worried, which I doubted.

And that left me sitting in a chair, holding a glass of bourbon I wouldn't finish. I had not reported a murder. I had kept my mouth shut about Rex killing Farley. I had denied I had any interest in Banks. And I had pulled a gun on a couple of amateur blackmailers and taken their goods.

Even if I hadn't already decided to leave the police academy, it was a fair guess that I wasn't cut out to be a cop. Too much was going on, and my part in it wouldn't pass the smell test.

If I had any sense, I would pour another drink, pocket Martin's money, and tell Street that there was no need to find the jockey now. Then I would take off my clothes, crawl under the covers, and sleep until I got my nap out.

But since I don't have any sense, I called James Lee Penny and told him I was coming to see him in the morning.

At the gym.

Chapter 20

PENNY HOOKED HIS THUMB through the loops and wound the wrist wrap tight. He unhooked the loop from his thumb and grunted. He slid onto the bench, his back placed carefully so that as he gripped the bar, his shoulder blades moved toward each other and the arch in his back got higher as he pulled his feet closer to his shoulders. I stood behind him, ready to help if needed.

"Don't grab the bar unless I tell you to. If I'm in trouble, I'll let you know."

"You got it."

He took a deep breath and moved the bar off the rack holding it. He took another breath, tightened his core, and brought the weight to his chest. There it rested for more time than I thought it should, though in retrospect it was only a second. Then, with an explosion of power, the weight came up. It was like a string was attached and some unseen being pulled it upwards.

"Rack it," he said, as I simultaneously pulled the bar back onto the rack.

"Impressive."

"I don't know how impressive it is. A lot of this is practice. You get good at what you practice. Don't you find that to be true?"

I thought about it. I used to drink a lot. Had a lot of practice at that and got pretty good at it. Everything else, it seemed I didn't do a lot of, except wander around asking questions. I wasn't sure how good I was at that. I just shrugged.

"That's what I find. You only get good at what you work at. I work at this, so I'm pretty good, I guess."

"You're good at this and you're good with horses. But you don't do either of these for a living. What else are you good at?"

He had taken off the wrist straps and tossed them onto the bench. "A little bit of this, a little bit of that makes the world go around." He looked sideways, up at me. "But you know the answer to that question already, right?"

"Let's say I heard you were in commerce. Of various kinds."

He turned to face me. "You could say that."

"Still in the horse game? Or are we talking humans?"

"It's all pretty much the same, isn't it? Humans. Horses. They go together."

"Just asking." I knew better than to press a man who might not want to answer questions.

"Simms tells me you're going to be a cop."

"That's what all the cops say."

"Sounds like you disagree."

"I don't disagree or agree. I don't have much of an opinion, to be honest." I pointed to my ankle, which was now back to regular size. "You saw the other day when I was trying to squat. I've got a little ankle issue that has to resolve itself."

"You squatted fine for someone who's never done it. Looks to me like if you really wanted to be a cop, a sprained ankle wouldn't keep you from it. At the very least, it wouldn't keep you from being clear about whether or not you were going to go back to the academy."

I guessed that was right. If I really was gung-ho, I would have no trouble saying so. But I couldn't just come out and say it, and it was becoming clearer by the day that I was done as a cop. Not that I ever was one.

"I don't really make you for a cop, so it's just as well."

"What do you make me for? I don't think I'm that easy to read."

"Maybe not for most people. But a lot of my success is based on being able to understand who's in front of me."

"What do you see, then?"

"I see a man who likes puzzles. I could see it Monday when you got in the rack to squat. Most guys, no matter their background, jump in and immediately do some version they think corresponds to the work. You didn't."

He stood next to the bench, crossed his arms. He was smaller than I was, shorter, and yet in any analysis, he contained more power and energy, standing still, than I ever did.

"I watched you watch Simms. You watched me too. Once you got in the rack, you did the best imitation of Simms I've ever seen. Right down to the way you flared your fingertip on your left pinky. Then, except for the depth problem, you went at precisely the same speed. The depth thing is just a matter of proprioception."

"Prior what?"

"Proprioception. It's the awareness of your body in space. Athletes have it."

"And I didn't?"

"Not for this movement. Not until it was explained to you. After that, you got great depth."

"And that tells you that I like puzzles?"

"It tells me that your default setting is to pay attention. Most people's default setting is to walk through life looking for something that confirms what they already think. You seem to operate on a different setting, that's all."

"Being in combat taught me to pay attention."

"That's not likely true," he said. "Lots of folks have been in combat. Some of them, maybe most of them, get out alive by luck. You had the setting for paying close attention before you got to Vietnam. That's why you do what you do."

"And what is it that I do?"

"I've heard you get yourself in situations where people have puzzles to solve. I can see that."

"Just on the basis of one workout?"

"Two if you count this one. But yeah, after an hour of watching you work, I could've told you in general what you did for a living." He uncrossed his arms and sat, beginning to rewrap his wrists for another set. "And you've got enough sense to look before you leap."

I waited.

"Look to see if someone's dry cleaner is working before you spill something on them."

"Ah."

"Yes. That's what made me check up on you. Imagine my surprise when Simms brought you in here." He lay back down on the bench. "Spot me?"

I took my place behind his head, standing on the rack's frame.

"When you've got four hundred pounds on the bar, you have to know you can trust your spotter."

"Seems like I'm okay by you, then. Since I'm spotting and all?"

He repeated the sequence as before. The weight went down and came up easily. I wasn't really a spotter. He didn't need me. Not with this amount of weight.

He sat back up. "You're fine, Jackson. You've got good sense. You know which toes not to step on and which ones to stomp." He gave me the side-eye again. "People tell me a lot of things."

"I'm just trying to make an honest buck."

"I'm not judging. In fact, there's always a place for people like you in my organization."

"Not sure that would help me at the academy."

"And I'm not sure you're going back. Be that as it may, you can call on me if you need to."

"I appreciate it, James Lee."

"And now that I know that you're a trustworthy spotter, I know I can count on you too."

I didn't say anything to that. But I was pretty sure I knew what it meant.

Chapter 21

When I returned to the apartment, a red light was flashing on my answering machine. It was James Lee. "Call me," he said, and he gave the number.

When I called the number, an unfamiliar voice answered. "James Lee? Yeah. Hang on."

I waited long enough to begin to think of hanging up when I heard James Lee's familiar rasp on the other end. "What are you doing later this afternoon?"

I could have told him I was going to try to find the medical examiner, but that would have been infinitely less interesting than something James Lee Penny could tell me. "Nothing."

"Good. You know the School of Mortuary Science?"

"The one on West End between Centennial Park and Vanderbilt?"

"That's the one. Be there at five this afternoon. A bruiser named Ronnie will meet you."

"A bruiser? He's going to give me a licking?"

"Ronnie's a sweetheart. He works for me. He'll bring you to me."

"Just you and me, James Lee? Or is Ronnie part of a committee?"

"Just you and me, Jackson. And maybe a couple of other guys. One guy in particular I think you might want to meet."

Five o'clock had a hard time coming. It was a long three hours. I made myself some coffee and sat in my rocker, staring out the window. You could see the change in the weather coming. First, the sun went away then the clouds turned from white to gray and then to black. I turned on the television to see if the weather gods had issued a tornado or thunderstorm alert, but if they had, the guys on WSM were keeping it to themselves.

My coffee was cold, so I made another. I could smell the ozone in the air, just the way I always did, even from my youngest days. It was a sign that you needed to get to the house before the rain came. Just as I sat down with a fresh cup, the bottom fell out of the sky.

It was four o'clock.

A hard rain has a way of washing the dirt out of the air and the dirt out of the street. And that smell after a hard rain?

I had a course in college, a botany course, that clued me in. I could always smell ozone still, just like before the rain. The prof explained that the lightning in a storm rips up nitrogen and oxygen atoms with a jolt of electricity, and the spare oxygen atoms will attach to oxygen molecules for an ozone party.

But there was more happening than that. The hard rain would cause oils on plants to hydrate and begin to be smellable again. And there are spores that, when conditions are dry, hold onto their smells, only releasing them and their spore pods when they're hydrated again. That's the earthy smell you get in the woods after a hard rain.

Like I said, there's a lot going on in your nose after a hard rain, but there's even more going on than you think.

Kind of like life.

The sky put on its color show in reverse, and by a quarter of five, the sun was out again, at least for a little while. I put on my windbreaker and headed toward Twenty-Fifth.

***

The morticians' school was an odd feature of the West End area. Snug with the Steak 'n Egg and the Vanderbilt Business School, it was the butt of all kinds of jokes among students. Or rather, it functioned as a kind of serendipitous excuse to make jokes about the quality of food at Steak 'n Egg or the difficulty of tests in the b-school. As in, that's why it had to be where it was.

I suspected the reality was that it had been there long before either and that inside, they made jokes about something else.

I knocked on the side door as instructed. When it opened, there stood a large man. He towered half a foot above my six-two frame, and his head was shaved. He wore a T-shirt with the single italicized word "bodacious," spelled with four a's, which could have referred to the enormous biceps the shirt could not contain. My guess was that he was a powerlifting buddy of James Lee's. Or that he really was hired "muscle." He had enough for sure.

He nodded when he saw me and jerked his thumb in a motion that said "get inside." He closed the door silently and got in front of me, checking once to make sure I was following. We went through the hallway, up a flight of stairs, and into a second-floor room that simply said "Conference."

"Boss is in there," said Ronnie.

"Thanks, man. Okay if I just go in?"

"Knock once. Then go in. Don't want to surprise him."

Spoken like a man who didn't like surprises either. "Cool."

I did as I was told and went in. James Lee was there, as was a man with striking green eyes, the kind that see everything and give nothing away. He stood next to the window, leaning against the wall, motionless except for his eyes.

At the table with James Lee was a nondescript little man. If I said he looked like he had no distinguishing features, that would be false. His nose was a little crooked. His eyes were slightly too close together. And his ears were just a hair larger than they should have been. But the point was not their minor deviance from normal. The point was that in combination, he could have passed you on the street, and you couldn't have described him five minutes later. He was the kind of guy who blended in then disappeared.

James Lee shook my hand. "Glad you could come."

"What's all the *Spy vs. Spy* stuff?"

His laugh was raspy too. "You mean the side door and escort?"

"At the mortuary school, no less."

"No less, indeed." He motioned for me to take a seat. "Metro keeps a tail on me. If they knew we were meeting, that could be a problem for you." He smiled.

"We've met before."

"That's at the gym. This is different. And I have a fellow traveler."

The nondescript man bowed his head. "Timothy Day. Of San Marcos, Florida," he said, as if I might mistake him for Timothy Day of Sanibel Island.

"A pleasure, I'm sure." I turned back to James Lee. "Who's your other friend?"

"That's Reese Lockman. He helps me out sometimes. I thought it might be good if you two laid eyes on each other."

I waved toward Reese. He didn't move. Didn't smile. Just watched me.

He unnerved me a bit. I turned back to James Lee. "What gives?"

"Is your interest in the matters at Harpeth Ridge still active?"

"If you mean the horse and the jockey, you know it is."

James Lee stroked his chin and murmured something indistinct. Timothy Day of San Marcos played here's the church, here's the steeple with his hands, his mind seemingly absent from what I was saying.

"Why don't you have a way to connect the facts?" He leaned back, his fingers still on his chin.

"I hope it's not a case of seeing something because you're looking too hard for it."

"You think you're looking too hard?"

"Might be. But nobody else is looking."

James Lee's eyes were the kind of blue that didn't change, no matter what he was thinking. Not cold but cool. Calculating. The kind that could hide anything.

But they weren't hiding anything just now. "I got to thinking about my pal, Tim, here."

Day's steeple came apart, and he was attentive again.

"What made you think of him?"

"The dead horse. You see, Tim's known by his nickname. Aren't you, Tim?"

"Indeed, yes. A well-known name is better than a business card."

"Tell him your nickname, Tim."

The nondescript man beamed. "Timothy 'the Sandman' Day," he said. "San Marcos, Florida."

"I take it you aren't involved at Harpeth Ridge?" James Lee was asking a question. It was clearly rhetorical.

He made a dismissive noise with his nose, not quite a snort but almost. "I have never worked in Tennessee. There wouldn't be enough business here. Florida and California are really the only places with the kind of volume I require to be profitable."

"You can't travel to other locations?"

"I really prefer not to. It's hard to raise a family if you're gone all the time."

"Give him the lowdown on how it works, Sandman." James Lee was attentive. With a wiggle of his eyebrows, he invited me to pay attention too.

"I used to do three horses a week. With the owners paying up to thirty-five large for each 'hit' as part of an insurance scam. Been at it for about ten years now."

I exchanged glances with James Lee. "That seems pretty lucrative."

"Oh yeah. I got paid more for killing horses than a lot of people get for killing people. All's I got to do is to electrocute the horses. Easy as pie. Doesn't leave a trace. All you got to do is attach one end of a wire with an alligator clip to its ear and the other to its ass and then plug it into a wall socket. Sizzle. Bang. Done."

"How fast, Sandman?"

"They go down immediately. One horse dropped so fast in the stall, he must have broken his neck when he hit the floor. Call me a sicko, but it's quick and painless. And here's the beauty: the only sign is a singe mark." He winked at me. "And nobody's ever looking, so they never see it."

I leaned back in my chair. "You told me you had a sense of things, James Lee. You really think something like this could have happened at the country club?"

He put his elbows on the table, the hands coming together, first as if in prayer then interlocked. "I told you that you were a puzzle man. I don't know what happened out there. I'm just giving you a piece from another puzzle that has the same theme. You might need it. You might use it. It might not fit. Puzzles are funny. They're really hard to get started.

"This is when we just need to pick a piece. It doesn't matter which one. Just pick one. Then start looking for one that looks like it will connect to it. If it doesn't, then try the next one and the next one.

"Keep going one piece at a time until you find a piece that fits. Then do it again and again. Before you realize it, you look up and there are a bunch of pieces hooked together and a picture beginning to take shape. We need to remember that we can only put one piece in at a time. Concentrate on that one. If it doesn't fit, then pick up a different piece and focus on it.

"But you know all that, don't you? You know it intuitively. It's the way your brain works, my friend."

I knew when I didn't know enough. "I appreciate it, James Lee. I really do."

"Then here's one more nugget. Word is out that maybe the horse had a foreleg issue."

"That's old news."

"Not if it's bad enough to kill the horse for the insurance."

I sat without speaking. There was a lot to digest.

"It goes without saying that Tim here had my assurance that you would not repeat his story. In any form."

"It goes without saying." Even if it hadn't been James Lee Penny who was asking. Even if he wasn't asking at all, but telling.

Chapter 22

WHEN I WAS A kid, the family made a weekly trek into town. It wasn't as if we needed much at the grocery, our operation being subsistence farming at its root, but we did need some staples: flour, salt, sugar. And since we three kids did go to school with other kids who were not from subsistence-farming families, we had our share of "needs," which is to say products that were not needed at all but which were nevertheless desired, mostly of the candy, chips, and soda pop variety. To their everlasting credit, our parents didn't deny all those creature comforts but rather made each of us choose one and only one to buy.

My sister went for Goo-Goo Clusters, and my brother always wanted grape Nehi. My preference was for the small six-ounce bottles of Coca-Cola, a preference that made both my siblings shake their heads. "You could get a twelve-ounce bottle, Knucklehead," my brother would opine. He never understood that the smaller one had the same amount of syrup as the bigger one. More bounce to the ounce, as a later song about an entirely different subject would have it.

Those trips into town were notable for another reason: a trip to the county library, where we were encouraged to check out whatever we wanted. The only rule was that if you checked it out, you had to read it, and there was no more checking out until you'd read all you'd taken.

It was as if you could go to the buffet as often as you wanted, but you could only go with a fully clean plate.

That behavior made my siblings wary about books, and both got their one book each week and read it. My brother was especially good at finding small books that he could finish in an hour in case he hadn't gotten to the book until breakfast on Saturday. He could polish it off if he got up early and read before breakfast. My sister tended toward picture books and then, later, books of photographs, the better to skim through.

But not me. I wanted books I could read, and I wanted more than one. From earliest times, I checked out two, three, four books, reading them ravenously all week, only to return to get more the following Saturday. I was that kid who read beneath the covers at night with a flashlight, and I read in the morning, waiting for the school bus. I read in the outside toilet, and later, when we had one, in the bathroom, sometimes so long that someone would come knocking to make sure I hadn't fallen in.

It wasn't until later that I found the library had all sorts of other treasures hidden away. Magazines. Journals. And people who knew how to help you find things. It was like a cathedral to me, the sort of place where priests and priestesses could open the doors of whole different worlds.

Of course, an eight-year-old doesn't think in those terms. But I always treated those Saturday missions with a sense of awe at what I could find. And six ounces less of Coca-Cola probably got me there faster.

So it was no surprise that my instinct led me to the JUL, the Joint Universities Library, to see if I could learn more. Timothy the Sandman told an interesting tale, but it was only, so far, one that could be told in Florida. And he claimed he wasn't working in Tennessee. I needed to find out what such a horse would look like in a postmortem. If I could square that with what Day had told me, I might get somewhere.

I ended up in the reference department, where I found an older woman in a polka-dot dress. She looked like she'd been there all day and didn't look that pleased to see me. I'm scruffy. She should have been used to that, though. Some of the undergrads, and all the graduate students except the ones in business and law, were the same way.

"Yes," she said. It wasn't a question. It was a statement.

"I'm sorry?"

"Yes, I can help you. That's what I do."

"What I'm looking for is a little obscure."

"That's what I do. The obscure is not a hobby. It's my occupation."

"Equine electrocution."

She wrinkled her nose, then made a sound that must be the sound of a librarian laughing. The face looked right, but the sound didn't carry. "That is obscure. Power lines falling in a meadow, that sort of thing?"

"I'm more interested in the postmortem aspects of horses who've been electrocuted."

"Like autopsies?"

"Exactly like that. Where would I find those?"

She was already standing and moving away from her desk toward shelves on the back row, behind her desk. I walked around the enclosed perimeter that half-walled her work area from the rest of the reference room. "I have some indexes here that will tell us the names of our journal holdings. We should have a few." She took a book off its shelf and looked over her shoulder at me. "You'd have better luck at UT. The vet school will be much more extensive in its holdings."

"If it comes to that," I said. "I don't have time to drive to Knoxville."

"Nobody does." She had the book open and was running her finger down the page. *"Journal of Equine Science, Equine Science Review, Southeastern Studies in Equine Science.* I think all those sound like they could be possibilities, don't you? I assume you only want the peer-reviewed ones?"

"Why wouldn't I want all of them?"

"Because the non–peer-reviewed ones are titles like," she looked back down, *"Farm Journal,* or, here's one, *Horse Husbandry Today.* I don't think they'll have a lot of interest in the effects of electrocution on a horse's corpus." She made the laughing face and funny sound again. "Horse's corpus. Hocus pocus." She shut the book. "Sorry. You have to make your own jokes in here. Nobody ever gets them."

"Where are those journals housed?"

"They'll be in the five hundreds." She scribbled on a pad and tore off the sheet. "Try these on for size. You may find others in the general area that are interesting too."

I took the sheet of paper. "Thanks. You've been a big help."

"Come back if you get a cold trail. There's other magic we can do. Hocus pocus and all that."

***

Research is not hard work. Oh, it's intense and puts a strain on your eyes and your ass, but what it mostly requires is doggedness, a kind of patience and persistence that defies description sometimes. I often found myself, as a college student, sitting in the library or sitting with a book on a college lawn, silent, for hours, immersed in the search for something, oftentimes something I didn't know existed. It's merely a matter of sitting, patiently, waiting for the thing to appear.

It's not a lot different from having spatter vision in combat. Relax your eyes. Let your field of vision go wide and a little blurry. You can't look too hard or you'll miss it. You can't see it if you're too specific. You have to be open to it when it comes, especially if it doesn't look like what you thought you were looking for.

You have to understand that you may not know what it is. And you may not know, even when you do spot it. You may have to let it bloom for you.

I was in an empty carrel in the oldest part of the library, surrounded by stacks of bound journals. I had taken the most recent three years of all three journals, scoured the titles without finding much, then carried to the carrel ones from further back that had titles that could be helpful. None of them, so far, had produced anything like a list of things to look for when horses die by electricity.

Probably because it doesn't happen that often. Maybe because it never happens unless Tim "the Sandman" Day does it.

If horses don't die of electrocution, save for Day's ministrations, the thought occurred to me: is electrocution ever used as a homicide method with humans? I mean, I've always heard that you shouldn't plug your radio in next to your bathtub, but do people kill other people that way? And if they do, would there be postmortem studies of that?

I went back to the reference librarian and told her what I'd found, or not found, and asked her my question.

She frowned. "I've always heard that too, but I don't recall ever reading that someone tossed the radio into his wife's bath.

"But then, it's probably because it'd be so easy to cover up the deed. You know, 'I came home, Officer, and found her. I don't know how many times I told her not to have that radio there.'"

"You have a fiendish mind." Polka dots and all, I thought.

She didn't seem to disagree. "I just meant that maybe it doesn't happen, and the story is there to remind us. Just as we say, don't touch a hot stove."

"Human studies in electrocution?"

"Equine science is one thing. Fairly compact field. Even more compact set of peer-reviewed journals. Humans? Humans are endlessly fascinated by themselves and study themselves in every way imaginable."

"Where to start, then?"

"In this case, the easy answer is the library at the medical school." She wrote on her pad again and ripped off the top sheet. "Dinah Sharp is a friend of mine. Used to work in our reference department. Tell her Connie sent you."

If Dinah Sharp had played football, she would have been a fullback, the kind that never got the ball, who always blocked for the star halfback. But she looked like the type who, if you gave her the ball against a stacked defense on the goal line, she could get you the touchdown.

I wouldn't have been able to stop her, that's for sure. She was a hair under five-eight, but she looked like she went about two hundred and twenty-five pounds, with wide shoulders and thick ankles. She could have been forty, but she could have been sixty. And she looked at Connie's note and broke into a smile.

"Oh, I miss that place."

"She said you could help me. I'm looking for postmortem studies that would describe the effects of electrocution on the human body." I was handing her the ball.

She nodded as if her play had been called. "Got it. Give me just a minute, and we'll get you where you need to be."

When she returned after a few minutes, she said, "You want to start with the *Journal of Medicine and Forensics*. That appears to be the go-to journal. Here's the location. Let me know if you need anything else."

Touchdown.

I thanked her.

***

Over a period of several years, the subject of electrocution came up occasionally. It seems that scheming husbands do not regularly toss electric radios into their wives' baths but that all sorts of workers, including a surprising number of electricians, get themselves knocked into the next world by electricity. It would be fair to say that working with electricity seems to be the best way to get killed by it.

There were also a fair number of struck-by-lightning stories and studies, but those had more to do with traumatic effects afterward or, more often, the lack of traumatic effects at all. None of the journal articles had exactly what I wanted.

Because I didn't yet know exactly what I wanted. Time to let my spatter vision work.

I turned away from the *Journal of Medicine and Forensics* and began to walk down the rows of bound journals. Some had titles that conveyed their stature, ones with single-word titles like *Physiology*, and others that declared their parentage, like *The Boston Journal of Medicine*.

When I came to a short set of journals titled *Forensics and Pathology*, I collected them and carried them to a study table. In one was contained a grisly study, complete with graphic pictures, of a suicide electrocution where the high voltage had ripped skin down to the bone. In the last paragraph, the authors noted, "Moreover, victims of low-voltage alternating current may have no inner electrical burns; this possibility makes the diagnosis of electrocution difficult. Specific evidence of electrocution in the internal organs is often lacking. Therefore, distinguishing between autopsy findings with prior postmortem imaging might help to clarify whether electrically induced injuries are present—even for low-voltage incidents."

I looked around and saw a white-coated medical student. I waved to him and walked over with the journal. "Sorry. I'm not a student. Could you translate something for me?"

"Depends. What language is it in?"

"It's in Medical. Or Forensic. I don't speak either."

He laughed. "Let me see." He looked at it. "Pretty straightforward. Household current doesn't usually leave signs in the internal organs. But some kinds of more powerful imaging might find some." He handed the journal back. "From the looks of it, their guy didn't need much imaging. One look and you can tell what happened to him."

"No kidding. So, you wouldn't know where I could find out more about this imaging?"

"Sure. I was just about to take a break. Come with me."

Very helpful, these medical types.

He pulled a tome off the top shelf. "*Postmortem Studies: An Index.*" He rifled through until he got to the E's and pointed it out to me. "Here you go. All the electricity-related postmortem studies in peer-reviewed journals. There for the taking."

"Amazing."

"Not really. Best medical library in the Southeast. Better than Duke's. Better than Emory's."

But that wasn't what I meant. What was amazing was that I was about to find what I didn't know I was looking for. I could feel it.

The prize was in the fourth article I looked at. It was a simple set of sentences, and it confirmed everything the Sandman said. "Electrocution causes damage to the tissue through which the electric current passes, and the only gross evidence is the electrical mark localized on the skin at the point of contact with the conductor. In some cases, the current mark is not detectable, and the diagnosis of death due to electrocution is a challenge for forensic pathologists."

Plain enough. Nobody would have seen the marks because no one would have been looking for them.

I went to thank my medical-student guide, but he was long gone. So was everyone. I had outlasted them. The building was about to close. On the way out, I stopped and dropped a dime in a pay phone. I reached into my shirt pocket and extracted Bud Simms's phone number. After four rings, he answered.

"It's Jackson," I said. "I've got some information."

"You can't still be working on Fool's Trade. Michael Martin won't like it."

"He can't keep me from looking around."

"And you've found something?"

"I've found something to look for. But I'll need your help."

He was silent. "Okay. My office. Tomorrow at noon. I hope you've got something."

I've either got something. Or nothing. "Thanks, Bud. Tomorrow."

Chapter 23

When I returned home, my favorite Metro detective was sitting on the step, waiting for me. Flood was persistent. He was a good detective. He didn't take no for an answer.

"That your little red Mercury out there?" It didn't seem his style, but it didn't belong on the street.

"I want to talk to you."

"If it's going to be a long conversation, come on up. You know the way."

He stood up, and we were inches apart. "What I don't know," he said, "is why you are acting this way."

"What way is that, Flood? All I'm doing is what anyone would do, somebody who is sidelined by a bum ankle."

Once inside, I lit a cigarette. Flood's ubiquitous toothpick moved from side to side in his mouth. I could usually tell if he was agitated by the speed at which the toothpick moved. He wasn't agitated. Not yet. The toothpick migrated to one corner and stuck.

"Why are you hanging around with James Lee Penny?"

"You're right to the point today."

"You know who he is, right? Working out in a gym is one thing, but you know who he is."

"You tell me, Flood. Do I know?"

The toothpick crossed the meridian line. "Don't be a smart-ass."

"Don't be an ass, then."

"All right. Maybe you don't know. Penny is the kingpin of the Dixie Mafia in Nashville. They're involved in a lot of illegal activity."

I played dumb. "What's he into? Prostitution?"

"No. Give him credit for that. As far as we can tell, he steers clear of anything in the skin trade. That includes porno."

"What else is there for the Dixie Mafia?"

"He is a horse guy, right? So it stands to reason he knows a lot about the ponies."

"Gambling?"

"That's part of it. But you know how that goes. If you're in for a penny, so to speak, you're in for a pound."

"What's that mean, Flood? That gambling leads to other stuff? The way weed is supposed to lead to heroin?"

"We know a lot. We just can't make it stick."

"Why not? You seem to know all about it."

"Knowing and proving are two different things, Jackson. As you well know." The toothpick made its way back to its original spot. "That's why we have a tail on him. That's how we know you've been talking to him."

"I don't get it, Flood. Why expend department resources on what, at best, is a pretty small-time activity. After all, there's not that much action in Nashville. Hell, there's not even a track. You've got the Sweepstakes, but that's one afternoon a year. It's an awful lot of resources to put on one guy for one day a year.

"If it was one day a year, Penny couldn't make a living at it. He'd be small-time. And he makes book on a lot more than horses."

"Such as?"

"His outfit runs the entire sports book in town. He'll take action on Churchill Downs or just about any horse race in the country. He'll do basketball, baseball, football, college and pro."

I whistled. "That seems like an awful lot of action for one guy."

"It's not one guy. I told you. It's Dixie Mafia." The toothpick moved then stopped. "We don't know for sure, but we think his action probably is in the high six figures every year."

"That's a lot of bets," I said.

"That's not the bets, Jackson. That's his take from the bets."

If James Lee Penny's take-home on the betting was a half a million, I didn't see why he needed to do anything else. "Sounds like a brilliant career. Sort of a savant."

Flood twitched. "Maybe not a savant so much. More like a genius. A criminal genius."

That was not hard to believe. James Lee was very well read. He knew a lot about a lot of things. And it wasn't hard to believe, after meeting the Sandman, that James Lee had tentacles stretching all the way down to Florida. A well-read, unusually bright person who understood people. It wasn't too hard to believe he could be a criminal genius of some sort. I didn't say any of this. I was willing to let Flood tell me what he knew. And he was eager to tell me.

"That's why it's really important that you stay away from this guy."

"Not good for my budding police career, right?"

"You don't seem to be taking that problem all that seriously." The toothpick moved rapidly to the other side of his mouth.

"To be honest, I'm having second thoughts about all that anyway."

"I sensed that. You seem not to be feeling the brotherhood all that much. Care to explain?"

"I'm not sure I'm cut out for the uniform. That's all."

"Not everyone is. But you? You're made for it. You like helping people. That's what it boils down to. That and the family. A group of people you can count on. Who always have your back."

"I'm not sure that appeals so much to me, Flood. Not the way it does to you."

"What's that supposed to mean, Jackson? That you are a loner? That you don't need backup? Because I can tell you, buddy, you would be wrong about that."

I put out the cigarette, stubbing it in the ashtray. I broke off the bright coal at the end and watched it slowly extinguish.

"Here's the thing. When I was in the army, I felt part of something bigger. The way you're talking now. Like it was a brotherhood of sorts. But once I got in-country, once the bullets started flying and the unit changed personnel every month, it felt less like a brotherhood and more like, I don't know, an arrangement."

"You can't tell me you didn't depend on your squad," he said. "You had to."

"I certainly did depend on my fire squad. Without those guys, you couldn't get from day to night."

"That's what I'm talking about," he said. "That kind of trust. That kind of brotherhood."

"That was war, Flood. That was mortal combat. Kill or be killed."

"Just like it is here. Some days."

"How do you get from helping people, as you say, to mortal combat? Just how do you get that far in a sentence or two?"

The toothpick moved rapidly, side to side. "You're twisting my words. There are bad people out there. And some days, we're all that stands between good people and bad people."

"I don't dispute that. There are bad people everywhere. Hell, Flood, the first time I met you, you were pretty sure I was one of the bad people. And to tell the truth, I wasn't so sure that you weren't on the wrong team too."

"You know what they say. You have to break eggs to get an omelet. Sometimes it's necessary. Turned out okay for you in the end."

"Turned out okay for me in the end because I made sure it turned out okay. That should tell you something."

"It tells me that you can be a good cop. Just like I'm a good cop. As long as you keep your head screwed on tight. And stay away from the people you should stay away from."

"See, there's the thing, Flood. People giving orders. It's not a thing I do."

"You got to be kidding. You took orders in the army. Didn't you leave as a sergeant? You gave a few orders too, I bet."

"I did what I was told. That's true. You do that. If you want to stay out of the stockade. You also do it for unit cohesion. If one guy ignores the order, the other guys are in danger. But out here in the world, you get to make choices. And I think I'm choosing not to be a cop."

He slammed his fist on the table and bit the toothpick in two. "I went out on a limb for you. I vouched for you. I even got you the damn scholarship, the posting that follows. You are already a Metro cop." I think if he could have brought himself to spit on the floor, he would have done it. "You don't have any say-so over this anymore. You're in too deep."

"Saying I'm in too deep, my detective friend, makes Metro sound like a criminal enterprise."

"You know what I mean."

"I do know what you mean. That's the problem. Words mean things. You think you can describe going to work as combat. You want to tell me who I can and cannot see. It sounds like a criminal enterprise. Our side against their side. Pretty simple."

"You're going to be on the hook for thousands of dollars. Last time I looked, you don't have thousands of dollars."

"You can't help yourself, Flood. Now you sound like you're blackmailing."

"I'm just saying what's obvious. You'll owe us a ton of money if you quit."

"And what's gonna happen to me if I don't come up with the money? The same thing that happens if somebody doesn't pay off James Lee Penny? A few broken bones? Or just time in jail?" We were nose to nose. "See what I mean?"

Flood had turned red. He jiggled his foot. Shards of the toothpick were in each corner of his mouth. They were jiggling too. "You're not making any sense. What's gotten into you? I just came here to tell you that you're ruining your career, and probably your reputation with the force, when you're seen with a known felon."

"Does the felon know he's involved in combat with Metro?"

"I don't care what he knows. He's on the wrong side."

"I go by my eyes and my ears. Right now, all my evidence says that he's just a weightlifter who knows about horses."

"And what I tell you goes for nothing?"

"I go by what my eyes and ears tell me."

"Yeah? See what your eyes and ears tell you when the shit hits the fan, then."

Flood left in a rage, slamming my brand-new door so hard that I thought the hinge at the top might come loose. That's the one I wasn't sure about when I screwed it in, after all.

Don Mercer, my Vanderbilt cop friend, likes to ask me on the regular what is it that makes me want to deliberately provoke people. And my answer is always a version of the same thing: I don't have any control over how they react to me. And that's true.

Everyone chooses to react. Or they choose not to control their natural reaction. It may be that my natural reaction is to be deliberately provocative, to say the one thing that I know will make the other person explode. Maybe I don't do it on purpose. Maybe I just want to say what's true because it seems to me that the true and the deliberately provocative are frequently one and the same thing.

Why is the truth so provocative? Why is it that the one thing we can't stand to hear is the thing that must be said? Is it because as a species, we are much more comfortable living where we know what we know, and no one ever says anything different? We spend our lives in search of brotherhood, we say. But what we mean by that most often is that we seek the comfort of those who will not say what we do not believe to be true.

We seek not truth but comfort. Even if that comfort comes at the expense of the truth, even if that comfort is a bundle of lies.

I have no idea if the Metro police brotherhood believes things that I do not. I do believe that many of them are wise and good men and women and that even Detective Bobby Flood has a lot on the ball. I'm just not sure I'm cut out for their company. And I'm pretty sure that they would not like mine.

Most of the time.

Chapter 24

It was raining again, the kind that makes you think you could sleep a little longer, a little further under the covers. I tried that for a minute but felt guilty then felt cold and wanted coffee, a shower, and warmer clothes, preferably something waterproof.

I made short work of my morning rituals, put on the closest thing I had to a raincoat, stuck my .45 in the pocket, and looked out the window. About fifty feet east of the mouth of the Buckets' driveway, there sat the same bright red Mercury I saw the day before. I didn't believe Flood would be staking me out. I couldn't see Penny needing to stake me out, and if he did, he'd do it professionally, not in a bright-red flare that said, "Look at me!"

Fortunately, my reno job in the apartment had provided me with a back door, a set of steps to the ground, and a newly worn path out to the street where I always parked the Impala. Just because I live in a garage apartment doesn't mean I park in the garage.

I pulled out past him and honked, just to make sure he saw me.

He did.

We did a line dance down to Elliston, then right. I led him down West End past Centennial Park and then further down until we were past the bars near Thirty-First. Then I turned left and circled back, leading him all the way to Hillsboro Village before I hung a left on Twenty-First and headed back toward the hospital.

I could imagine him thinking I was either a bozo or giving him the business. I'm not sure he was all that competent as a tail, so he probably just thought I was a bozo.

I finally hung a right on Broadway, parked in front of Mack's Cafe, and went in. The guys at Mack's have seen me enough to not think a whole lot when I overshot the men's room and went through the kitchen, out the back door, where there's always a couple of dish-washers pitching pennies and smoking. I slid past them and exited on Twenty-First, rounded the corner, and saw my boy in the red Mercury, cigarette smoke curling up through the driver's-side window.

If he saw me edging up to the Merc, he gave no sign of it. His gaze was trained on the big pane of glass that said Mack's Cafe. I could see that the plunger was up on the back seat, passenger side, so that was where I made my move. Thumb on the push button and I was inside the Merc in the backseat, my Colt nestled against his throat.

"Since I don't know you, and I don't know if you're carrying, you'd be smart to put both your hands on the steering wheel."

He did it, but he took a little more time than he should have.

"If you're going to answer my questions that slowly, we're not going to get along."

He looked into the rear-view mirror. "Who're you? I don't have a problem with you. What's your problem with me?"

"My problem is that you're following me. You were following me yesterday." I scratched his ear with the muzzle of the gun. "I don't like to be followed."

"You got it wrong, bud. I'm just about to go in for breakfast here."

"Unless this car's got a mind of its own, you're following me. It's not hard to notice a bright-red Mercury Comet. Not in this town."

He didn't move. His hands didn't shake, and he kept his eyes on me in the mirror.

"But I'll tell you what. If you want to have a bite of breakfast inside, come on in. If you've got a good enough story, I'll buy."

And with that, I jumped out of the Comet and walked back inside Mack's, gun safely stowed in my raincoat pocket. I took a booth in the back corner and nodded when the waitress asked if I wanted coffee. When I saw the driver come in the door, I whistled at her and signaled for two cups. By the time he sat down, she'd delivered two hot mugs. "Scrambled with bacon. Gravy biscuits, too." I looked at the driver. "You?"

"Just coffee for now."

He had small eyes that never rested. They darted constantly and seemed to take in the world in little jets of information. He wore a straw Panama hat with a red band. Just like the red Mercury, it made him obvious. He wasn't a natural tail.

"My name's Bennett. Lindell Bennett. People call me Lindy. Maybe you heard of me?"

"Not by any of those names."

The coffee was a little hot to drink, so I lit a cigarette and pushed the pack toward him. He had small hands that went with his small eyes, and they darted just the way his eyes did, grabbing the pack and pulling a cigarette free. He took my Zippo and lit the cigarette, his darting hands depositing the lighter back before I could offer it.

"I've worked up and down I-65 for a while. Louisville. Nashville. Birmingham."

"And what do you do for a living, Lindy?" I was certain he didn't follow cars for a living.

"I move freight. You know. Liquor. Cigarettes. That sort of thing, if you know what I mean."

"Sure." I wanted to ask him if he was freelance. Or if he was part of James Lee's crowd. But I figured he was going to tell me that. "Are you following me because I look like I've got a crate of cigarettes in my trunk?"

He cracked a smile. "Nah." He put out the cigarette like he didn't care for the taste. "You're not in the game. I know that."

"Then enlighten me, Lindy. Why's a guy like you following a guy like me?"

He leaned forward and put his hand by his mouth, as if somebody could read his lips and he didn't want them to know what he was saying. "I got something to sell."

"I buy my Marlboros at the A&P. Legally."

"Don't be a punk."

I leaned forward to meet him. "Then don't be a shitass, Lindy. Get to your point before you ruin my breakfast."

"You know LaRae?"

"Farley's redhead? What's she got to do with this?"

"Dempsey ran out on her." He raised his eyebrows and tilted his head, as if what he said would make everything clear. When I looked blank, he leaned closer and whispered, "He took all of Farley's gate. The girl's got nothing."

"Lindy, this is all interesting. LaRae is, in fact, interesting if you're interested in that kind of girl. I'm not, and now Dempsey's not. I'm assuming you are. Interested, that is."

The darting, beady eyes settled on me. He exhaled like a man who had had enough but didn't know exactly how to say that without getting a gun in his face again. "She needs money. And we got infor-mation." When I still looked blank, he said, "Information you would like to have."

The waitress brought the plate of breakfast, steaming hot, just the way I like it. I thanked her.

"What have you got that I would give you money for, Lindy?"

"Richard Banks."

"The jockey?"

"That's the one. Interested?"

"Banks ran off with a woman. That's what Metro says, anyway."

"Banks is dead." He looked pleased with himself. He congratulated himself by sipping from his coffee, pinky finger aloft.

I put the paper napkin on my lap and picked up my cutlery. I sawed a bit of biscuit off, swirled it in the sausage gravy, and put it in my mouth. There was just enough grease and cream in the gravy to make the mouthful divine. There was just enough salt to make it sing. "Who cares?" I picked up a strip of bacon. Crisp. Delicately greasy. Perfect. I took a bite. "Banks isn't my problem. Dead or alive."

"I'm not kidding. Banks is dead."

"Tell it to Metro, then."

His hand flew across and clamped on my wrist. "Look, bud, I know you're in this. LaRae said so. She said you were supposed to find Banks."

"I was supposed to find gambling receipts and blackmail pictures. I did that."

"Yeah, that's right. But you were supposed to find the jockey. And LaRae knows all about him."

"She says he's dead, right? No concern of mine anymore."

"But you were supposed to find the jockey."

"He ran off with a woman. I told you."

"I know. Vera Peele."

That got my attention. I put the fork down. "Did she kill him?"

"You'll have to pay up to get any of that." He leaned back now and unbuttoned his coat. He reached for the mug and drained the coffee, all in one gulp. "Two hundred gets you everything we know."

Chapter 25

LINDY BENNETT WASN'T SO pleased with himself that he dumped the information right away. "Come back to LaRae's apartment tonight. About seven."

And the little man left as quickly as he could, no doubt partly because he had to report back to LaRae that I would take the bait so they could set the hook.

For whatever it was they knew.

I finished my breakfast, a second cup of coffee, and the sports section of *The Tennessean* that someone left in the booth closer to the door. Once again, I was amazed that a city with an SEC team in it could spill so little ink on the school's athletics. If I'd had to depend on the newspaper to know what was happening with Vanderbilt athletics, I'd have guessed there were no teams over there at all.

The day passed slowly. Bright sky turned to gray, and gray turned to storm clouds. By the time I got to LaRae's apartment complex, the sky had turned black, and the air smelled like ten thousand raindrops getting ready to pound the earth all at once.

I got to the building's entrance just as the first drop landed, leaving a wet spot three inches wide. Two seconds later, the earth was covered in buckets of the stuff.

She opened the door, the chain still on.

"Oh. It's you."

"Who were you expecting? The mayor?"

She took the chain off and muttered, "Just get in here."

LaRae receded into the room, her black outfit telling me that she was on her way out. A small black suitcase held the middle of the living room, and she fiddled with a hat straight out of Mata Hari.

"Going somewhere?"

"Lindy said you had a couple of hundred you'd give for the information. I want it."

I reached into my pocket and waved a couple of hundreds at her. "Where is Lindy, anyway? I thought he'd be here. Thought you two were a team now."

"Forget Lindy. I want the money. Then I'll tell you what I know."

I walked over close to her. Her red hair was beginning to fade. It was a dye job or a rinse. It made me wonder how much of her act was the same. "Tell me first. I don't like paying for things I haven't seen yet."

LaRae considered the sequence. Without the info, there wouldn't be any money. Without the money, she couldn't do whatever it was she wanted to do. She gave in.

"Fine." She flounced onto the sofa.

I continued to stand, the bills in my hand.

"Fine," she repeated.

"The sooner you say it, the sooner you get the cash."

I thought she might say "fine" again, but she didn't. "Me and Dempsey were taking a ride a couple of weekends ago. Out I-40. We were thinking we'd go out and ride the rides at Opryland, maybe."

They didn't seem the type for that, but who knows? "Sounds like a Sunday outing."

"Yeah, except when we got there, we saw Vera Peele getting in a car with somebody that wasn't Willie Peele."

"Banks?"

"Not a chance. This was Art Spatz. You know him?"

"Sure. That's the guy that hangs around the stables. Big guy. Hard to miss." I didn't say where else I'd seen him.

"Well, they got into a car in the parking lot just as we were pulling in. That doesn't look right to us, so we followed them."

"Dempsey's good at that, is he?" He'd have to be better than Lindy.

"It's about the only thing I can find that he's good at." She crossed her legs. Whether she was a redhead or not, she tanned like a Brazilian.

"If I'm paying you by the word, two hundred's coming cheap. Get to the point."

"Spatz was driving. They went east on 40 for a while, then got off at the Mt. Juliet exit. Dempsey stayed pretty far back. A mile or so outside of town, there's a dirt road that heads off into the woods."

"Are you about to tell me there's a love nest back there? That Spatz is taking her to where Banks is?"

"Banks isn't out there. But you're pushing me. Let me tell the story."

I waved the bills. "Time's money, LaRae."

"The road is called Lebanon Dirt Road. There's an old Esso station back there that looks like it was deserted a while ago. And in another quarter mile or so, there's a frame house, looks like a shack, really. That's where Spatz dropped Vera Peele."

"Are you telling me you followed close enough to know this but not close enough that Spatz saw you?"

"I'm telling you, Dempsey is good at this. Our car was in the woods, and Dempsey went up in the dark to have a look-see. He said the lights were on and a radio was playing. He didn't hear any voices."

"Just Vera and Spatz."

"No. Spatz pulled out while Dempsey was gone."

"How do you figure it, LaRae? Banks is supposed to have run off with Vera. Vera is conveniently out to Opryland with Spatz so that you and Dempsey can see them. Then Dempsey slinks up and says she's in the shack. How the hell does that compute?"

If LaRae could see the two hundred evaporating, she didn't show it. "It's not my fault we stumbled on them. Lucky for you is what I'd call it."

"Why is that?"

"I'm telling you where she is. Either Banks is there with her, in which case you get your jockey. Or he's not. Which could mean something else."

"Or it might mean you're setting me up." I held the cash toward her, too far for her to reach. "Lindy said Banks is dead. Why?"

She grabbed for the bills and missed. "All right. There was nobody there in the shack with her. She's just out there cooling her heels."

"Why, LaRae?"

"Best we could figure is she's a decoy. For somebody. Maybe Banks. But maybe somebody else, like Spatz."

I gave her the bills. She grabbed them like they were a starving man's meal, snapped her clutch open, and put them in. The purse snapped back violently.

Chapter 26

I DROVE EAST ON I-40 until I got to the Mt. Juliet exit. I half expected to see some commemorative sign saying that Charlie Daniels
welcomed me to his fair city. All I got was a thirty-year-old Clabber
Girl placard, six by three and washed out by decades of the elements.

The weather wasn't kind. It rained again, though the cats and dogs
had already fallen, and we were now in the kittens phase of gentle rain.
The hiss of water under tires was wearing on the spirit nonetheless,
and I was glad to pull off the interstate.

I had the windows of the Impala cracked now to let in a little fresh
air, but all I was getting was the back and forth of the wipers and the
skein of water every time somebody passed me.

Mt. Juliet wasn't much of a town. There was a main street with
tributaries off it, like a small-time river with streams that went
nowhere. The main drag was Highway 171, and you could call it Mt.
Juliet Road while you were in Mt. Juliet, but it would be called some
other town's name when you were in that town. It's just the way things
were. Nothing really belongs to you, even if you call it by your name.

Off the interstate, there was a cluster of businesses catering to
the traveler, the sort of truck-stop-and-cheap-motel clusters you see
everywhere. Further in, going toward the town, you began to see little
frame houses, sad wooden buildings with something rusting in the

front yard or appliances on the front porch, which then gave way to neater, more put-together and well-mowed places closer to town. By the time you got to the town center, you were faced with the inevitable IGA or A&P and a local Rexall drug store and the obligatory seed-and-feed operation. There was nothing in Mt. Juliet proper for Charlie Daniels to sing about.

The dirt road LaRae told me about was easy enough to find but hard to notice in time to turn. I failed to do so and caught both right-side tires in a ditch that was half full of water. I tried in drive, then I tried in reverse, but the Impala was hung. I could hear the undercarriage scraping against the gravel on the side of the road.

I got out in the light shower of rain and inspected my situation. Even if I had a young man or two equal in strength to me, I don't think we could have brought the Impala fully up onto the shoulder. No, this was a job for a tow truck with a good lift.

I walked down the road, knowing that LaRae had identified a shack. I found it a hundred yards further down.

It presented itself as the sort of outbuilding that somebody had bought for the sole purpose of storing something that was a nuisance at their own home. Or maybe it was where the tractor and the bushhog lived when they weren't out in the field, mowing. In the mist and rain, I could just make out a glint of light underneath the side boards. I heard the whine of a machine, not quite a table saw but something like that.

I banged on the door to the shack, and the sound stopped. Then the light went out. It was as quiet as the moment after sin.

I hit the door with my fist twice more. "I saw your damn light. Open up. I need some help."

"Main road's a half mile back the way you came. Go get your help there." The voice was low in volume but came with its own rumble of thunder. "I ain't of a mind to help anybody I don't already know."

I pounded the door again. "At least let me use your phone. I'm getting soaked out here."

The bolt shot back on the door, and the business end of a double-barreled shotgun came out through the opening. I backed up, hands in the air. "No need to get hostile, friend. My car's in the ditch out here."

The shotgun stayed where it was. "No need for you to be an asshole." His voice lilted, mocking. "Friend."

We stood like that for what seemed a full minute. "Let me try again, sir. I'd like to use your telephone, please. Unless you have a tow truck."

The shotgun didn't move, but a different voice came through the crack in the door. "Let him in. Let's see what we can do."

The light came on, and the door opened. My friend with the shotgun was a tall, skinny man that, if he'd had the right kind of pants, would have resembled the country singer Stringbean. He had a scar on the side of his hand that was raised and red, angry like it'd been there a while and was still allergic to the world.

Sitting at a table behind him was a man in a checked shirt and a loosened paisley necktie. He didn't look our way but had returned, now that there was light, to considering a spread of solitaire in front of him. It was Art Spatz.

He played a card on the lines in front of him. "Go ahead and start up the tow truck. See if you can't pull him out of the ditch."

The taller man unbreeched the shotgun loudly. "Do what?"

"You heard me. Go pull the man out of the ditch." He looked up briefly. "You can pay him, right?"

"As long as it's not more than twenty."

Spatz went back to his game. "Twenty's a fair price for sure. Seeing as how you don't have much choice all the way out here."

Stringbean cussed under his breath. He unbreeched the shotgun and set it on the table in the middle of the room. He snatched an old corduroy work coat and shouldered into it. "I'll be back."

"Come and sit." Spatz motioned with his hand without taking his eyes off the game. "You can explain why you're here on such a rainy night." He looked up and smiled. "Please sit down and tell me, Mr. Trade."

Chapter 27

THE WEIGHT HAD FALLEN on the back of my neck. Or something had. And where it had fallen raised a welt and creased me like a hot poker would. The last thing I saw was Spatz's face leering at me, one eye cocked and his mouth pulled to the side, as if he was about to say something. But he didn't, and the sensation I had was of falling, heavy and to one side. And then there was just darkness.

When I woke, I was in a different place. It was warm, and the light was dim and a radio was playing Patsy Cline's "I Fall to Pieces." I usually hear that on a jukebox in a bar, so I never really got the sensuousness of her voice on that song. Just then, though, it felt like a poultice on my head. It wasn't loud and penetrating, just soothing and low.

I tried to move and felt several parts of me crack like I'd been put in a grinder the wrong way. I started to rub my neck, then realized my hands were tied. I stretched my neck a little. I was careful. It didn't matter. It hurt like hell.

"Good evening." The voice came from a woman near the dimly lit gooseneck lamp. I could make out smoke curling into the lamp, circling the light bulb. Near it, a water glass was filled with half-melted ice that had turned whiskey pale yellow. "How do you feel?"

I tried to move myself into an upright position. I had little luck until I managed to swing my legs over the edge of the couch, which had the effect of swinging my torso and head into the correct position for sitting. It also had the effect of pressing whatever cranial fluid was floating in my head against my skull bone.

It hurt like hell too.

"I've been better." I could smell enough of the cigarette smoke to feel like I wanted one. I looked around the darkened room.

"They've gone. Although they really wanted to stay until you woke up." She got up and walked toward me. She was tall but not willowy. The kind of woman who can do a full day's work on a farm and still have plenty of energy. Knew a few growing up. Not many. As much as men said they wanted a helpmate like that, not many could handle one like that. She looked solid.

"What do they want with me?" I squinted at her through the smoke. "Here's a better question. Why did they do this to me?"

She didn't say anything but took the cigarette and put it in my mouth, letting me get a lungful of smoke. I could taste the lipstick on the filter. Then she took it and walked toward the light. "I don't know how you found this place, Trade, but it'd be better for everybody if you hadn't." She stubbed the cigarette out in the ashtray. "Now we're just waiting for them to get back. To do what they're going to do."

"And what's that?" My own smoke was flowing back into my face. "Vera?"

She turned slowly, almost as if her eyes were surveying the room as she turned. "What did you say?"

"Vera Peele. Wife of Willie. Paramour of Richard Banks, according to the police and everyone who says they know." I felt behind me. The rope was tight. "Where is Banks anyway, if you don't mind my asking?"

"You're in a big enough fix, Trade. I'd let it be."

"If I'm in this deep, how much deeper could it go, Vera?" I was working at the rope quietly, but nothing was getting looser.

"Why chase out here? The horse is dead. Richard doesn't have a mount anymore. You don't need to find him." Her eyes flashed. "And I haven't seen him in a couple of weeks."

"You ran out on Willie. That's the word."

"Maybe I'm just taking a break. It's none of your business anyway."

I looked around the room. It had the feeling of a place put together on the fly. The couch didn't match the chairs, and neither of them matched the coffee table. It reminded me of my place before the reno. Early mid-century flea market, with a side of Grandma's cast-offs.

"I made it my business, Vera. I don't like people that lie to me then use me."

"Well, join the club. It doesn't matter whether we like it or not."

Her voice had descended from angry to resigned.

"That's right, isn't it? Willie does what he wants to. The jockey's in the way of his payday. He kills the jockey. Then the horse is about to be discovered. He kills the horse. Or Spatz does. And you and me, Vera? What about us?"

"They won't kill me."

"You sure they won't? You only know everything that's been going on." I waited, but she didn't budge. "They don't know how much I know, and yet they're coming back to kill me. What special treat do you think they've got planned for you?"

"I'm not afraid of Spatz."

"Sure. He's just the guy who follows the orders of your husband." I managed to get just the barest of distance between my wrist and the rope. "But let me ask you this, Vera. Are you afraid of Willie? After everything he's done?"

She spun and strode into the other room, coming back with a butcher knife. At first, I thought she was going to slit my neck, but she jerked her head and said, "Turn around while I cut you loose."

I did as she instructed. "Was it something I said?"

The knife sliced through the rope, and my hands came around. As I moved them into their accustomed position, I could feel the unnatural stretch the front of my shoulders had felt, and my head throbbed again.

"You need to get out of here. They'll be back any minute now."

"What about you, Vera? When they see the rope cut, you'll get the same treatment they had planned for me."

"You're too smart for your own good, Trade. Get out while you still have the chance."

She stood there, this tall, smart, and assured woman, married to a guy who was a rat. A fraudster. A killer and who knew what else. Her eyes looked tired now, and she slumped against the door.

I looked outside. If she wanted to sacrifice me to Spatz, this would be one way. But it didn't feel right, didn't feel like she was sending me to my death on purpose. "Come with me?"

"I'll take my medicine." She looked up, her eyes still tired but defiant. "And I'll take yours too. Go do whatever you have to do."

Chapter 28

VERA KILLED THE LIGHTS inside, and the dark outside was pitch. The rain had stopped, but it had left behind soil that sucked at my shoes. My neck still felt like it had been knocked into a new shape, and my head throbbed.

But my head was clear on one thing. Vera wasn't Banks's paramour. That story was one that Willie had fed to Metro. It kept them from looking for Richard Banks, but only if Vera was gone too.

It had setup written all over it.

My car was still on the tow truck's hoist. I opened the passenger side and checked the glove box. The handgun was gone. No doubt that was Spatz's doing too. He had all my money. He had my gun. And since he'd knocked out whatever sense I had in my head, he had that too.

I crab-walked to the trunk, keeping down in case Spatz picked this minute to return. With my fist, I popped the place next to where the key went in, and the trunk lid cracked open. I leaned in, flipped over the blanket in the back, and extracted the Browning I kept there. I was glad that Spatz hadn't figured the old Impala would give up its secrets without a key. He had a key, after all. But I had *the* key.

The box of cartridges was in the spare wheel well. I grabbed five and loaded the Browning.

I was running in a kind of stooped run to the side of the shack when the headlights caught the rise of the road and shot their beams above me. The beams flashed once at the house as if Spatz was signaling Vera. I was lying on the ground, as low as I could get without getting the Browning soaked. He killed the engine.

I didn't move. Neither did Spatz. The car sat there, the hood sizzling as the cooler mist made contact with the hot metal. I caught the glint of a lamp bulb in the far window. Vera must have pulled the draperies to the side so that the light showed.

Spatz picked that moment to open the car door. He rose like Bigfoot out of the driver's side, and Stringbean clambered out of the passenger side. They both stood still, staring toward the shack.

Spatz reached inside his coat and drew a gun. Maybe it was mine. I couldn't tell in the darkness. He motioned with his head for Stringbean to circle around the shack.

They had figured something was skewed. Maybe it was the lights. Maybe it was Vera not doing something she should have. Whatever it was, they were playing it cool and careful.

While Stringbean went around back, Spatz got behind the car door. "Let's cut the shit, Trade. Let Vera come out. Then we'll talk."

I was behind him. I had the perfect line of sight, and I brought the Browning up, ready to fire.

"Don't be stupid, Trade!" Spatz shouted, and his voice died in the night air. No echo and no resonance.

He put the gun on the seat and shuffled out of his coat, rolling up his sleeves. "All right, smart guy. Let's see how you like what happens next."

Before whatever was next in his mind, though, there was the sharp and unmistakable report of a gun. A dry, chapped snap, with the faintest of echo. They all sound alike, and none of them sound the same. I could have guessed that was mine.

Had Vera tried to escape out the back? Had Stringbean shot her?

Whatever Spatz was thinking, he didn't think it out loud. He crouched close to the ground and took cover behind a black walnut tree whose spreading branches drooped enough to provide something of a barrier between him and the shack.

I still had a clear line of sight. I thought about pulling the trigger.

Before I decided, though, I thought I saw movement to my left, ten feet to the side of Spatz. I say that I thought I saw something, but it was more that I had a feeling, the way you had a feeling in Vietnam, when something you couldn't see was about to go down.

Besides, my head was throbbing. My eyes were barely attached to my head. I probably couldn't see or feel much of anything.

Spatz was low and crouched. I imagined what he might be thinking. What had Stringbean shot? Who? And where was he? Those were the things I'd be thinking.

I realized I was gripping the stock like I was trying to strangle it. *No way to shoot*, I told myself. *Relax. Breathe. You've got the jump on him.*

Just then, I heard another shot. Spatz stood as if to run and fell over, reeled, and rolled onto his side. The gun in his hand sat as lifeless as he lay.

Stringbean must have seen him and mistaken him for me. I kneeled and took aim. Wherever he was, I had an approximation. And I had more firepower than he did. If I had to move away, the Browning had plenty of range as long as I could get a bead on him.

I waited like that a good two minutes. That feeling in Vietnam, the one where you were sure that Charlie was just out of your line of sight but that he could hear your very thoughts, that was the feeling I had. Head throbbing. Eyes hurting. Nothing working the way it should.

"Get down, Trade."

The voice was behind me. Quiet. Insistent. Familiar.

"I'm your friend. But don't turn. Put the rifle down, barrel to the ground."

I didn't move. "If you're a friend, don't disarm me."

"Take this." He pitched something that fell to the ground in front of me. A Colt 1911. "That's yours. Both Spatz and his flunky have a slug in them from that."

"I don't understand."

"I took it out of your glove compartment. Good thing, too, because they looked for it. Nobody knew you had a deer rifle in the trunk, though."

I started to turn.

"Don't turn around. The Peele woman will tell the truth, that they ambushed you and were going to kill you. You got loose and you got the drop on both of them. It's self-defense. Open and shut."

"And you..."

"I came here to make sure you got out of this alive. Glad I did. If you blew them up with that buck stopper, it might be hard to explain. This seems a little more believable."

"Don't I know you?"

"A friend sent me. Kind of like a spotter. To make sure you got back for the horse business." He paused. "I'll call the sheriff when I get out to the highway. Until then, I'd check on the woman if I were you."

I kept my eyes forward. One of James Lee's boys. And there was only one who would work the game like this. "I appreciate the help, brother."

But he was already gone. There was nothing behind me but the night.

Chapter 29

For a guy with a big bruise on the back of his neck and a headache that just wouldn't quit, I was doing okay. In another life, I might have started the day with a double shot of bourbon, eaten a couple of Krystals, and carried metallic coffee in a paper cup half the morning before throwing the cold caffeine down my throat all at once.

But that was before. Now, I had an apartment I could look at with some satisfaction, if not a little bit of pride. I had a proper percolator to make coffee in. And my refrigerator held eggs that weren't too old and bacon that hadn't reached that stage of age where the grease is already coming out of the slices on its own.

In short, I got up, made coffee, and enjoyed my bacon and eggs, staring out the back window into a greenspace that had appeared seemingly overnight. Spring rains have a way of doing that. One day, you're looking at the dregs of winter; the next day, every leaf in creation has made its way to your world.

In this world, even the bruise and the headache were bearable.

And since it was bearable, I had driven the newly towed Impala downtown to visit with Eustace Montagne. At his request.

He motioned for me to sit in the chair in front of his desk while he listened on the phone. He muttered sounds that probably told the person on the other end that Eustace was listening, but the mutters didn't give anything else to hang on to. When he finally got around to saying an intelligible word, it was "Okay." Then, "Goodbye."

He stared at me, a kind of fatigue crossing his face. "You had quite a night, I hear."

"You get around, Captain."

"You may think I'm the guy who got promoted until he was out of his depth, but I was a pretty good cop. If you want to know the truth, I still am."

"The last word I associate with you is 'loser.'" It was true. The word I associated with him was "sharp."

"Anyway, you're clear on Spatz and Dinkins."

"Dinkins?"

"The man who ran the tow service. Seems they had a nice little chop-shop operation going on there. Kind of a way station before the stolen cars made their way down to Soddy Daisy for the final chop."

I shrugged. Stolen cars weren't a thing for me. How they'd got to be one for Willie Peele, I couldn't tell.

"How'd you find her? Vera Peele? Who gave her up to you?"

I told him about LaRae. I told him about Dempsey and Lindy Bennett. I left Martin out of it. I left the horse out of it.

And, of course, I left the guy who did the actual shooting out of it.

He leaned back in the wooden chair until it creaked under his weight. He looked at the ceiling. "They're not as smart as they think they are."

He waited to see if I would bite. I didn't.

"Spatz and Peele." He lowered his head, looked at me.

"How's that?"

"We knew they were out in Wilson County. Knew Peele's wife was out there."

He was cagey. I appreciated it. "Knew Banks wasn't there?"

"Pretty sure he wasn't." The creaking of the chair stopped as it reached its limit. Montagne couldn't stretch it any further. "Pretty sure the whole he-ran-off-with-her was just a lie. Something to keep us sidetracked long enough to get away with something."

I let the conversation sit there. I watched it sit there.

He made the chair screech. "Maybe you think I'm carrying water for Peele."

"Not you. Not for him. He's not big enough." I was thinking of James Lee Penny. He was big enough. But Montagne wasn't carrying water for anyone. He was too sharp.

And Penny's bunch wasn't part of Mt. Juliet. Except at the end.

"Let me tell you something, Trade." He finally leaned all the way up in the chair. It made a different sound coming down. Not a creak. More like a groan. "You're in the clear on this. I wanted to see you to make sure we're okay, the two of us. If you turn out to be a Metro cop, you don't want me to think bad things about you. And I don't want you to think bad things about me. Understand?"

"Sure. You want us to be on the same page with each other."

He pushed away from the desk with both hands and stood up, walked to the window. "We still don't know about Banks. Maybe he's just blown town."

"I doubt it."

"Yeah. I doubt it too. But what are you going to do?" He hitched up his pants leg and leaned one butt cheek onto the windowsill. He peered down at the street. "Peele figured he was primed to be the suspect, so he had Spatz take his wife out of town with a stupid story. He figured that would create some space, some time."

"And in the meantime, somebody would find Banks?"

"Something like that." Montagne turned his shoulders toward me, and his head followed. "Except you got in the middle of it, and Spatz lost his mind."

"And that's it?"

"Unless you're going to keep looking for Banks. But Trade?" He uncurled his body off the windowsill and rose to his full height. He was a bigger guy than you'd think. If there hadn't been lamps in the office, he'd have turned the room dark by standing in front of the window. "You seem like an honest guy. Things always happen around you, and lately, you've started to play rough."

"You don't want me to shoot back?"

"All I'm saying is that you seem all right. You might even make a good cop. But you need to cash in whatever chips you've got on this one and get out of the game. There's too many dead people since you got involved."

"Don't worry, Captain." I rubbed my neck. "After last night, I've had it with the whole bunch."

"Good. Rest up. Take a vacation or something."

I got up. I knew when I was being dismissed.

"And Trade?" Our eyes met. "Never forget. They're not like us."

"The criminals?"

"Them. And the rich folks too. Leave them be."

Chapter 30

Screw it.

I went back to Mt. Juliet.

Call me crazy. Call me single-minded. Call me anything you want, but Banks was somewhere. I had a hunch he was dead and buried.

And I was willing to bet he wasn't far from where they'd buried him. Once buried, the dead don't tend to move.

I parked by the tow truck garage and set out to explore the woods behind it. I had my cane hooked on my arm. I didn't need it. I had a short-handled spade that would serve as well. Plus it would dig.

My life as a kid was spent in the woods. Just after daylight, you could still feel dew on the small tendrils of forest plants like bloodwort and lizard tail. At dusk, in the middle of summer, you could feel the leftover heat that had barely made it through the canopy to the forest floor. At night, amid the calls of crickets and frogs, you could almost smell everything that had happened through the day, from turtle tracks to rabbit pellets.

No matter how good my sense of smell, though, nothing matched the smell of my beagle. Frisky was a dog who became a detective in the deep of the night, every aroma setting him on a chase that led to treasure. Frisky always found a thing buried, a creature forgotten, just underneath the leafy cover of the acid silt. Sometimes the carcass of a bird, sometimes the leg bone of some small animal, left behind by the hawk who consumed him. Frisky found them all, their smell rising just above the ground, just high enough for his attentive nose to find them.

I didn't have Frisky or his nose. All I had was the ache that comes when you know there's a body out there somewhere that used to be attached to a person. The person was dead. And the only way to prove it was to find the body the person used to live in.

The woods had begun to dry out, but my ankle still knew there was plenty of moisture in the air. It sat like lead on my leg and refused every attempt to do more than drag the foot along like an unwilling participant.

Fifteen minutes into this reluctant dance, I caught sight in the corner of my eye of a ridge of dead leaves. When I pushed at them with my spade, I was met with the sweet smell of fresh earth, the kind of rich, wet aroma of dirt that has been recently turned.

It was Spatz that buried him. You could tell because even the shovel marks were violent, random, furious. As if he was angry because the ground was too hard. Or not hard enough. It didn't matter. Nothing suited him, and nothing made him happy. Nothing except the cold, violent expression of distaste for the world.

The body was about eighteen inches down. I know how it goes when you dig a hole. It feels much deeper than it is because it's always harder work than you thought it would be. I could imagine him in the moonlight. Maybe he had just the shovel. Maybe it wasn't even the right kind of shovel. Maybe he had the flat-bottomed kind better designed to scoop corn off a metal floor and pitch into a hog trough.

But even if he had the right kind of shovel, the one with the pointed beak and the ledge for your boot heel? Even that would have been hard going here, before the last week's rain made the soil softer, the going easier. Before that, the dust would have quickly given way to hard pack, not red clay like they have down in Georgia but a kind of brown loamy soil that gives way easily enough to the subsoil, a yellowish-brown clay about eighteen inches deep. That was where he stopped because, past that, the layer gets dense and almost like cement.

That told me enough about Spatz right there. Perfectly happy to do the unthinkable. Until it got a little too difficult, and then he looked for a shortcut.

Typical mindset of a lazy criminal.

I limped out to the Impala, drove to the truck stop on the highway, and phoned the sheriff's office. They told me it'd be a while before a deputy could answer the call.

"That's fine. He's dead. He's not going anywhere."

The dispatcher went silent for a few seconds. When she came back, she told me to meet Deputy Liddell when he arrived. ETA was fifteen minutes.

Then I called Parker Street, told him I'd found the body that had started the whole mess. He did some quick math then said he'd have a check waiting for me at his office.

And then I limped back to the burial site and waited for the deputy.

Spatz, or whoever, had wrapped the body in black plastic and surrounded the plastic with lime.

"Trying to keep the smell down until later, I reckon." The Wilson County deputy was older than the usual deputy sheriff. He looked like he'd seen a thing or two. "Farmers bury livestock that way sometimes. They're trying to slow the decomposition down enough so that you don't get overcome by the smell."

"Same with the plastic?"

"Probably." The deputies who'd arrived with Liddell had opened up the plastic and slit it all the way down. There, looking asleep and not much the worse for wear, was a young man, mid-thirties, brown hair and mustache. "You come looking for him. Is this him?"

I had never seen Richard Banks in life. You can't always tell from a corpse what the life inside them looked like as it walked on the earth. But it certainly should be Banks.

He was clad only in boxers. Boxers with the Union Jack.

Chapter 31

THE MEDICAL EXAMINER'S LAB was a study in contrast. The lab itself was meticulously clean. It gleamed. Even the fluorescent lights seemed abnormally bright. The medical examiner himself, however, was disheveled. He looked like the scientist version of Detective Columbo. Everything about him suggested an inability to do even the simplest task. And yet, on closer inspection, every movement was precise, and no motion was wasted.

He pushed himself away from the table, snapped off his latex gloves, and adjusted his glasses. He looked at Flood and then at me. "I know why you're here. But who is this guy? I don't know him."

"Academy guy. Name's Trade. You'll probably get to know him soon enough. He ends up in the middle of everything, no matter what I do."

"Trade? Strange name."

"I didn't pick it."

"Fair enough. We all what got we got. And this poor sap," he said, pointing at the corpse, "he got what his DNA dealt him."

Flood looked bored. "It's natural causes?"

"Natural causes it is. Ventricular fibrillation."

"What the hell is that?" Flood picked his teeth with a toothpick. "Never heard of it."

"It's not common, but it's not rare either. There are two sides of the heart, one is the part that pumps blood out and the other is the part that pumps blood in. They work as a closed system. They're powered by electrical impulses, and the heart depends on that electrical stimulation to keep the rhythm regular and the blood flowing, so to speak." He looked over his glasses to make sure we were following.

Flood's eyelids looked heavy. "Go on."

"Fibrillation is when the stimulus gets off track. It causes the heart to beat erratically. The erratic impulse can come from either side, either chamber, of the muscle. When it comes from the aortic side, it's called a-fib. From the ventricular side, it's called v-fib. Our buddy here had v-fib."

Flood shifted his weight. He didn't look uncomfortable. Maybe just impatient. "What exactly does that mean, Doc? Is that kind of like butterflies?"

The medical examiner laughed. "If only. Butterflies would be nice. This would be more like a complete and utter breakdown of the muscle function of the heart. It doesn't take more than seconds, maybe fifteen or twenty, before someone in v-fib loses consciousness."

"Why would he lose consciousness?"

The ME gave a short, exasperated snort. "Because the heart would have failed, in that time, to supply blood the oxygen it needs for the body, specifically the brain, to do its job. If the brain doesn't do its job, the whole central nervous system shuts down."

I remembered a little bit of my human anatomy class. "And so if the central nervous system shuts down, no breathing, no heart beating, no nothing. Is that about it?"

The medical examiner looked at Flood. "The new guy's sharper than you are. Might want to put him on an accelerated path."

"Trying to do that. He doesn't cooperate very well."

"Anyway, that's the right answer. If you found him soon enough, you could do CPR, perhaps, maybe revive him, maybe bring him back. But this guy. He didn't have a chance."

Flood stretched, as if awakened from a nap. "You said DNA? This is a hereditary thing?"

"Could be. Or could be just the idiosyncratic defect in his heart. It's a shame, but it happens."

"This is your official finding? Natural causes?" Flood appeared awake and ready to leave.

The ME clinked his surgical scissors on the table. "Natural causes."

***

I admit it. I own it. There is a moment in a case when you suddenly realize that you are almost there, that you almost have the answer that you been looking for. In other times in my life, the answer had been just a little different than I thought it would be. But this time was different. This time, there was no doubt in my mind. A single person had been responsible for the death of a human and horse. And I knew who that human was. And I thought I knew why.

I spent the first part of the day letting Simms and the medical examiner get their information together. Both had assured me that they knew where they could find what they needed to find. Since the medical examiner was looking in his own files, I really had no reason to doubt him. And I had no reason to doubt Simms either. He seemed to know exactly what he was looking for.

I busied myself with tacking down some new flooring. It was the last little bit of renovation that was going to happen in the apartment. And while I had done all the work myself, I still felt the necessity to do it to a standard that the owners would appreciate. I spent a good bit of my morning crawling around on the floor, trying to make sure that I had not missed anything and that everything was sanded perfectly and ready to take a finish.

By the time I was done, it was time for lunch. I walked down the street and, forgoing habit, stopped at the little gyro place on Elliston. I had a very sloppy pita, and I licked the residue off my fingers. I finished my Coke and went outside. It's one of the few places on Elliston where there are places to sit.

I sat and smoked. I watched as people made their way down the street. All of them heading happily somewhere. Undergrads in top-siders and khakis. Townies, who looked at the undergrads and shook their heads. And people like me, people who fit into both categories or, perhaps, who really fit into neither of them. It was certainly true that the longer I stayed in Nashville, the less I felt a part of it. The problem was that I didn't much feel a part of anything, anywhere, anymore.

One o'clock was the appointed time for my call to the medical examiner. When I answered the phone, he was excited.

"I take it that you found the file," I said.

"I did, and it is just as I suspected. Or rather, as you suggested."

"Go on."

"The young man I told you about was a twenty-two-year-old. He was in good health and had no previous history of anything that would've caused his death. He had been electrocuted on the job. But his family wanted his body to be, as they used to say, used for science. And thus, we went to the trouble of a comprehensive look at the young man."

"And what did you find?"

"What we found was evidence consistent with an electrical death. Especially one low voltage. As you know, the high-voltage electrocution does all kinds of damage to the organs into the skin. Here, however, the damage is much more subtle, and we were looking for anything that would suggest to us that it was the sole cause of death."

"The electrocution?"

"Yes. That's right." I could hear paper shuffling in the background as he began to look for something else. "We did find that there was both an entry and an exit wound, one on each hand. The forefinger and thumb. He'd apparently grasped the wires exactly in the same way in each hand, and one had been the entry point for electricity and the other the exit. There was a burn in each place. Not a significant one, mind you, but certainly the sort of thing that we picked up on."

"So, what you're saying is the electricity came in with such power that it burned the skin?"

"Yes, exactly. That's what it does, and it exits the body in the same way. You see, the process of electrocution is that the electricity makes a full loop. If the loop is contained, it's a controlled system. The problem is when the human body becomes part of the system, the human body is not constructed to be able to handle that electrical load."

"That's very interesting, Doc. And I guess I knew it, in a way. What about the small capillary damage. Did he have that?"

"Indeed, he did. Both on the ventricle wall of the heart and in the lung tissue."

"Did he die because his heart stopped, or did he die because his lungs stopped working?"

"You ask exactly the right questions. And either could be true, to be honest. But in this case, because of the heart lesions, it was the heart. That means we can say that it was the electricity that caused the fibrillation that that ended up killing the young man."

"You said fibrillation. And Banks's death was caused by ventricular fibrillation."

"I knew you'd pick up on that," he said. "And that's right. This young man died of what I would characterize as ventricular fibrillation. The same as Mr. Banks."

"Help me out here. Doc. Make my day. Did you find that Banks had a burn mark on his body?"

"I went back and looked, just for you. And he had just one. He had a burn mark that was of unknown origin and so, therefore, did not cause any suspicion to fall."

"Where was the burn mark?"

"It was on his earlobe, just below the hairline. If I hadn't been looking really carefully around his head, I would've missed it."

"Doc, are you thinking what I'm thinking?"

"I don't know what you're thinking, but I can guess. And I'd say yes, it's entirely possible that Mr. Banks was electrocuted. The only problem is that there was not a second burn lesion. Just the one."

"I have a theory about that," I said. "But I'll keep that to myself for now."

"Do as you will. Let me know if I can help any further."

"Thanks, Doc." He had already helped more than he knew. And if I could just get the right information from a certain veterinarian, we would be moving in the right direction quickly.

Chapter 32

Bud Simms was deep in a pile of reference books. "What gives? You look like you're prepping for finals."

He looked up. "The final time to look at Fool's Trade. Have a seat."

I found a seat. It wasn't comfortable. It wasn't new. Nothing there was new to him, except for the instrument case that sat on top of the desk. Simms was the sort of man who didn't need the newest thing. He only needed the newest thing that made a difference. Another reason to like him.

"So, you remember that the postmortem suggested the cause of death was sudden cardiac failure. Sudden cardiac failure can come in all sorts of guises."

I thought back to the necropsy. "Yes, yes. I remember all that. Alphabet soup was what it was. EC. SCD. ABCDE."

"Don't be impatient, Jackson." He thought about wagging a finger at me, but it paused in midair. "Those findings are not inconsistent with a second look. In fact, the doctor went to some length to say that, as a commonality with other cases, such a thing could happen and maybe does happen quite often."

So far, I was not getting anything that I could use from Simms and his dissertation. "But you imply there are differences. What are they?"

"There you have the crux of the matter." He thumbed through a couple of pages and pulled one out. "Here is the key moment, the key passage in this little analysis." He pulled the paper up as he adjusted his eyeglasses and began to read. "The horse seems to have had a long-standing lesion which may have caused it to fail to perspire in an optimal way, at least for the purpose of racing. Whether this was because of rest and therefore the animal's relative lack of fitness or whether it was because there was a congenital difficulty is beyond the scope of this postmortem examination. It can be said, however, with fair certainty that such a lesion and the way it presents is consistent with a sudden fibrillation of the heart."

"Fibrillation. I'm hearing that word a lot, and it's making me believe that there is something wrong with the way the horse's heart absorbs the electrical impulse."

He nodded quickly. "That's true. Just as ours do, horses' bodies operate with an electrical current that tells the heart when to beat. It's a complex system. But to put it in simplified layman's terms, this postmortem, unlike the other one, which simply said that there was unexplained sudden cardiac death, possibly exercise induced? Well, this says that it was a cardiac event but that the cardiac event has to do with a fibrillation that is not necessarily exercise induced."

"And not necessarily naturally induced, either. Right?"

Simms inserted the page back into the sheaf, took his glasses off, and leaned back in his chair. "But here's a small, almost insignificant sentence that I found at the very beginning, during the physical description of the horse's exterior."

"I'm all ears. Let's have it."

He put his glasses back on and pointed so that he read where his finger went. "An examination of the horse's coat revealed a burn mark on the left ear."

Burn mark. I smiled, and he smiled as well.

"Here's the problem," he continued. "For electrocution to happen on a creature, human or otherwise, there would have to be a second burn mark. The circuit would have to be completed. We've got one burn mark. That doesn't exactly put me in a place where I can say with certainty that there was nefarious intent here."

"Nefarious intent? We're talking about electrocuting a horse. For insurance money. Anyone who would do that has lost their mind. Or their human decency."

"So," he continued, "I kept thinking about where another burn could be. And here's the sentence that matters: 'An unusual necrosis of the area around the horse's rectum, inconsistent with known types of injury. The pitted area was inflamed, as if it had been charred, and the tissue was necrotic.'"

He looked up at me, and if a vet could look triumphant, that's how he looked. "Do you see, Jackson? All the clues were there all along. We just didn't know what we were looking at because we didn't know what we were looking for."

Except I had known, thanks to the Sandman. I just hadn't been smart enough to put it all together. Until now.

"I owe you a beer, Simms."

Chapter 33

Even if you know, it doesn't do you any good.

Banks was electrocuted. Fool's Trade was electrocuted. Willie Peele was responsible for both, even if his boy Spatz had buried Banks and tried to bury me.

There wasn't a way I could touch them. And my Metro buddies couldn't care less. Banks was "natural causes," and the horse, well, was just a horse. Of course.

Except to the insurance company, but they would settle. They didn't need the truth. They just needed to make the actuarial tables come out right.

Spatz and Dinkins were criminals and, according to the story, I'd killed them in self-defense. Farley was dead, but he was a bookie, so no harm, no foul.

It's the sort of thing that can drive a man to drink.

Or it's the sort of thing that can make a man drive to see someone else.

James Lee Penny seemed happy to see me. He was dressed in a black singlet that emphasized his massive legs and wide chest. Many lifters have big bellies; the idea that more mass means you can move more weight, well, it's a fact. But James Lee didn't subscribe to that tenet, apparently. He didn't have a tiny waist, but he had a V-shape from his powerful shoulders to his midsection.

"You aren't dressed to lift." His face had no trace of doubt or distrust. Just a sunny demeanor and a ready smile. Like any of your average crime bosses.

"I've got a problem, James Lee. Maybe you can help."

"A lifting problem? One we can work out here in the open air?"

"More like a life problem. One I'd rather not have anyone else hear."

His sunny demeanor didn't admit a cloud to pass. "Sure. Step into my office."

The office was a small room with a desk, a washer, and a dryer. "Somehow I expected more."

"From a master criminal?"

I winced.

"I know what everyone says. Take it from me. People who make a living doing what I do fall into two camps: those who want you to know, want you to be impressed, and those who just want to get the job done."

I could see where James Lee fell.

"I appreciate your help in Mt. Juliet. I'm assuming…"

He held up a meaty hand. "Might have been my help. I can't say."

"Either way, it was appreciated. Maybe not needed."

"It was needed. Vietnam infantrymen with deer rifles aren't as sympathetic with juries as you'd think." He looked up at me, his eyes sincere. "You need to trust me on that. I know juries."

"Still. Thanks."

"Now, about your life problem."

I explained what I knew. How I knew it. He wasn't surprised. How could he be? It was the Sandman who'd started me down this road.

"In my business, you either take care of the problem or you let it go. Sounds like you're not letting it go."

"I can't."

"You've been paid."

"I don't know you, James Lee. You and I are very different."

"Not so different."

"Hell, I'm practically on the other side of the law."

"Or not. I know you, Jackson. You're not like them."

I'd heard that before. Already. From them. "I need to nail Peele."

"Pride? Or principle?" His dark eyes weren't accusing. Just asking.

"Principle, I think. Does that make a difference?"

"Only if you let it. As long as you know that it's a matter of principle and not about right and wrong."

"Why's that?"

"If you're going to act on principle, the ends justify the means. If you're going to get moral about it, that will complicate what you will allow yourself to do. Julius Caesar was killed on a matter of principle. It certainly wasn't a moral act."

"Are you talking history or Shakespeare?"

"Doesn't matter, Jackson. Same either way." He leaned against the washing machine. "If you're saying that getting Peele is a matter of principle, then you've got some options." He grinned like he knew a secret. "Let me make a phone call, okay? Go outside and look at the weights or something."

Ten minutes later, he motioned to me to come back in his office.

"You're in luck. Mr. Peele is a busy man who needs money. Without a horse in the race, he's free to spread his money around."

"Jet Pack, right? Rex Cameron's horse."

"It's a smart bet if you know horses. Cameron would have ridden her into the ground. That's what he did last year. But the new mount, Tamera Beasley? Smart. A real horsewoman."

"You know her, then?"

Penny flipped a coin and caught it. "Better than that. I trained her."

"Great. Then Peele has the odds-on horse and all his money on it."

"That's right. He's got all his money on what must feel like a sure thing. You know what that means, Jackson?"

"It means he's in like Flynn. Or Flint. Which is it?"

"Flynn. In like Flynn. The other is a James Coburn movie." James Lee knew all kinds of stuff.

"Anyway, he's got it made. Covered his bets, so to speak. Right?"

James Lee put the coin in his pocket and put the phone back on the counter. "That's one way to look at it. The other way is more interesting, though."

I didn't see another way.

"If you've got all your money tied up in a sure thing, what happens if the odds on the sure thing change? What if, suddenly, it looks like your money is on the wrong horse?"

"But it's not. You said so yourself. Best horse. Best rider."

"What if I told you, Jackson, that there exists a horse Jet Pack has never beaten. A horse that, in fact, has Jet Pack's number. Beats Jet Pack every time and always has."

"I'd say that horse is not in the Sweepstakes field."

"You'd be right. He's not." James Lee showed an entire mouth of gleaming teeth. "But what if he were?"

"Quit playing with me, James Lee."

"The horse is named Kid Galahad. He's a six-year-old gray who beat Jet Pack all seven times they raced as two- and three-year-olds. While Jet Pack came home to Cameron Farms here in Tennessee, and began her steeplechase career, the Kid was stabled at home in Florida. He races mostly down there now. But he's still got the old touch. He trounced Jet Pack last year in an Ocala steeplechase event." He raised both eyebrows and shifted his eyes to the left then the right in a pantomime of secrecy. "It wasn't close."

"And he's not in the sweepstakes here. So, big deal."

"You are far too trusting that the field is set. It's not. The death of Fool's Trade creates an opening. I think the race organizers would be very happy to entertain Kid Galahad as a late entry."

"And Peele?"

"I believe that Mr. Peele might be induced to acts of desperation." He gleamed again. "He might be tempted to repeat a death from natural causes."

Chapter 34

I WAS HANGING OUT with the wrong kind of people.

That would be one way to think of it. James Lee Penny was just enough of the wrong kind of people to know that Willie Peele had fifty large on the Cameron Farms horse, Jet Pack. Willie Peele was enough of the wrong kind of people to know that he had to win that bet. It was just too much money to lose.

Michael Martin was absolutely the wrong kind of people. He had a million dollars' worth of reasons to want to make sure that Fool's Trade insurance paid off.

So why did I feel right at home?

***

Bud Simms and I worked late that night.

"You sure about this?" For a veterinarian, he was a little timid when it came to arranging the death of a horse.

"It's just electricity, Simms."

"And you're not an electrician, unless you'd like to tell me something."

We worked without speaking for about twenty minutes. I was satisfied. "Give it a try."

"Not me. You."

"You're a chickenshit, Simms. You know that?"

"Better a live one than a dead one. It's your game."

I gave it a try. Willie Peele was in for a shock.

***

If there was a difference between Flood and James Lee, it'd be this: "You can't cheat an honest man." That's straight up philosophy from the king of the Nashville Dixie Mafia.

Flood had a different mantra. "They're all crooked. Bring 'em in and let the judge sort it out."

I was about to test the difference.

It was a simple matter to get Kid Galahad north. James Lee made a phone call to Florida, then Florida made a phone call to Harpeth Ridge. In two nights' time, a large gray gelding, once an elite flat-track racer and now a very serviceable steeplechase horse, stood noshing in a lovely west Nashville stable.

"That's one fine horse." He was something. Seventeen hands high. Muscles on top of muscles. The sort of horse who looks like he can run all day and jump over everything.

Bud Simms chewed a piece of straw. "Yep. You still sure?"

"You can't cheat an honest man."

I guess I'd made my bet already too.

***

My apartment was toasty from several days of April sun. I had a window open so that a nice cross breeze blew. In Nashville, you get two weeks of this before it gets too damn hot.

I picked up the phone. James Lee was on the other end.

"The book has shifted."

"That means that everyone knows. Kid Galahad is the favorite."

"It means something else, too. Willie is getting nervous."

"Tell me something, James Lee. We know what Willie is going to do. What would you do?"

"There's always something you can do. Have a talk with the jockey of Kid Galahad. See if he's somebody you can buy or at least rent."

"Willie won't do that?"

"It's not in Willie's wheelhouse. He doesn't deal with the humans, only the horses."

"What else?"

"Like I say, you could influence the rider. Or you could influence the race. Alter the course. But Kid Galahad races well on all surfaces and beats Jet Pack on them all as well. So there's no play there."

"You can't get to the rider. You can't alter the course. What's left?"

"Just what you already know, Jackson. It's all about the horse."

***

Flood was still pissed at me. But he was listening. "Makes sense?"

"Your theory is that Banks and the horse were both killed this way."

"Correct. And that Willie Peele is the guy."

"Even if you're right, there's no guarantee."

"I'm right. And I don't need a guarantee. I know how he's going to react. He doesn't have a choice."

"What if you're wrong?"

"Then you've wasted a night and I'll buy you dinner for your trouble. But if I'm right, you'll clear one homicide."

"Which isn't classed as a homicide."

"Even better for you. And maybe you'll close a couple more. You never know."

"For a guy who doesn't want to be a cop, you spend a lot of time doing Metro's work."

"That's not entirely true, Flood. I spend a lot of time doing your work."

"You're hilarious, you know that?" He uncrossed his arms, a sign that the conversation was over. "I'll be there. Let's hope you're right."

***

It was hard to know how grown men could be so quiet. Well, that's not entirely true. Flood was a cop who'd spent a lifetime on stakeout. And I'd been in combat, in Vietnam. I could be quiet. I guessed I was only worried about Simms. But he was a veterinarian. The horses were comfortable around him.

If Willie knew any of us were there, he didn't show it. He went to work, attaching one clip to the ear of Kid Galahad. The horse half rose, then got completely to his feet with a snort. Willie stroked his neck. "That's right, old boy. It's me again. Come to finish my job."

The horse settled and barely flinched when Willie attached the second clip near the horse's tail. Then, Willie unrolled the coil of wire and made his way toward the outlet in the corner of the stall.

It all came to this. I was right. I had known I was. But now, I had to hope that my electrical skills had been up to the task too.

"Goodbye, old buddy." Willie plugged the plug into the outlet.

And nothing happened.

Kid Galahad shook his head and swished his tail. I could almost believe he was trying to dislodge the clips. But I think he was just restless.

Willie unplugged then replugged. The outlet was dead.

And the horse was alive.

Just at that moment, I flipped the light switch. The barn was awash in light. Willie stood like stone. A man not given to quick movements, he wasn't moving at all.

Simms sprang from the next stall and checked the horse. Flood positioned himself at the stall's opening. I was already inside.

"You." Willie pointed his finger at me. He might have moved slowly, but he processed information quickly. "You set this up."

"Thanks for the demonstration, Willie. We have the autopsy on Banks. We have the necropsy on Fool's Trade. Now we have the motive and opportunity to match up with the means. You did all the work for us."

"You don't have anything."

Flood had the handcuffs out. "I think we'll let the District Attorney make the call on that. For now, hands behind you."

"I'll be out before morning."

"Might be." Flood was double locking the cuffs and making them just a little uncomfortable. "Not my concern."

Chapter 35

Martin was sitting in an overstuffed chair with pillows on either side of him. He looked older. He seemed tired. I couldn't tell if he was drunk, but he had a bottle on the table, and the glass was half full. Or half empty. I don't know how to handicap that kind of stuff anymore.

"Sit down, Trade." His voice was strong enough. It conveyed a certain disdain.

I wrangled one of those wing chairs and pulled it closer to his. The air in the room was stuffy, like an open window would have been an affront. The curtains were mostly closed, admitting but a little light into the room. The whole room stank a little of dead skin and bad breath.

He stared at me then reached for his glass and took a sip like it was medicine. Maybe it was.

"I don't recall hiring you to meddle with my horse business."

"Maybe not. But you're a smart guy. You knew I would."

"That's not what I paid you to do. I paid you to know better than to stick your nose in where it's not wanted." He took a breath, a sip, and then put the glass back on the table. "You found Peele out. I'm not sure what good that's done in the end."

I kept quiet. I didn't know what I wanted to get out of this interview, but an argument with the old man wasn't going to get me anywhere.

He continued in the same, flat voice. "It doesn't matter, I suppose. No more than it matters that you've found Peele out on the matter of Richard Banks. Parker Street has paid for that one, right?"

"Yes. Parker paid." I found myself suddenly wanting a sip of that bourbon myself. Not a good sign. "Is that it? Is that all you wanted to see me about?"

He closed his eyes as if he was too tired to think. His hand reached toward the glass but stopped in midair. "I should never have engaged you in this. Now everything is upside down."

"Not quite upside down." I licked my lips. They were too dry. The house was dark and fetid and humid, and my skin was crawling. My lips felt like they might crack. "I didn't do what you wanted, but Peele did."

"If you are insinuating that I put him up to all this, I . . ."

"You'll deny it. I get that." I leaned back and crossed my legs, hoping the change in posture would change how much I wanted that drink. "And I was able to nail Peele, but he'll have to implicate you. I can't do that. I know that."

I reached inside my jacket pocket, pulled out the envelope. "Here's your money back. I did what you wanted. I got the gambling receipts and, whether you know it or not, I did a little bonus work there too."

"Yes. I know about Imogene's little problem. She told me."

"So we are even. I did your work, but I did some work you didn't want." I tossed the envelope on his lap. "There's your money. Even steven."

He opened his eyes but didn't touch the envelope. "Why haven't you gone to the police?"

"What makes you think I haven't?"

"I have been in business a very long time, Trade. I can read people. You could have told the police everything you believe about me, and they would at least by now have paid a courtesy call. But they have not. No one has said a word."

I shook out a cigarette and hoped it would dampen the desire for a glass. "Do you remember what you said when you hired me? You left it to my discretion how to handle Farley. Well, handling Farley had nothing to do with handling him. It had to do with handling the indiscretions of people who were attached to you, one way or another." The Zippo flared; I lit up. "By the way, the police found Farley's body. He was buried not far from Banks. Probably by Spatz."

"Are you implying that all this is my doing? Again, I object to that."

"I'm not implying anything. I'm saying that I did do the job you assigned me to. It was pretty amorphous, and the instruction was pretty loose. It turned out differently than you wanted, and that's why the money is back in your lap."

"I'm not following you."

I gave up and crossed to where he was sitting. I took the bottle and uncapped it, then took a good hard slug from it. I looked at him, staring at me with a little disgust. I poured him a couple of fingers, then took the bottle with me back to the chair.

"No, you're not following me. Let me make it easy. You wanted me to scare Farley or pay him off. You didn't much care. He was just a distraction to you. The real problem was Banks. He had seen enough of the horse's foreleg problem to bet against the horse. And Cameron. He had an inkling too. But then Cameron did you a big favor. He took Farley out himself. Stupid, if you ask me, but he was a rash kid."

I took another swig. The bourbon was hot, and it burned, just like I remembered. I felt a wash of tension, and then I shuddered a little as the tension unwound. "Banks was dead, and you really didn't need me fooling around looking for him. So Peele and Spatz got the wife to disappear. It made sense. Banks was putting the moves on everybody's wife. Right?"

The eyes closed again. I thought he might have gone to sleep. Or passed out. But he hadn't. "Yes."

"Too many people knew too many things, even if they were dead. If they could find out, why couldn't I? Why couldn't anyone? So you had Peele kill the horse. It was neat. The insurance would pay off." I took another drink. "Or maybe that was the plan all along. Just collect the insurance."

His arm moved again toward the glass. This time, he took it. We took our medicine at the same time.

"But you stayed in the way." He centered the glass in his lap, both hands on it for safekeeping.

"I stayed in the way. I tricked Peele. He exposed himself. It's not like anyone had to grill him. He made it easy."

A long minute passed. Finally, he opened his eyes and looked at me. What gleam he had in youth or in his prime was long gone. He drained the glass and set it back on the table. Then he took the envelope and held it out toward me. "I want you to go away. You say you haven't set the police on me, and I believe you. For whatever reason, you seem honorable that way."

I took a swig. "Thanks. I think."

"But I would like to assure myself of your continued friendship." He shook the envelope. "Take this. And I will have another for you. Periodically. Think of it as a retainer on your good will."

I set the bottle on the floor in front of me. "You mistake me, Martin. I'm not honorable at all. I don't give a single damn about you and your horse nonsense. I didn't know Banks, so I can't say I got all that attached to him."

"Then what are you saying?"

"If I start trying to right all the wrongs that you fat cats cause, I'll be up to my ears in bullshit before nightfall." I stood then scooped up the bottle. I looked at it for the first time. Evan Williams. It'd been a while since I'd sampled that. I took another sip. The burn was gone. "And if I take your money, even if it's to keep quiet, it's the same as working for you."

I walked over and set the bottle on his table. It wasn't empty, but I'd made a dent. "You'd better keep it. My silence is still good. If they get to you, it won't be from me."

My boots made very little sound on the wood of the floors. Parquet. Some kind of design in the boards. Very nice. Completely unnecessary. "But you and I know, Martin. And unless I miss my guess, that's enough."

Enough for me, because I knew the truth.

Enough for him? Time would tell.

Chapter 36

The maid didn't say anything, but her look said that she wasn't going to get in my way. "I'll be in the living room. Tell Mrs. Martin I'm waiting for her."

It was a good ten minutes before the door opened, and Imogene walked in as she always did. A confident stride. This time, she was wearing a tennis skirt, a sleeveless white knit top, and impossibly white tennis shoes. She carried a delicate bone china cup of coffee. She stopped and stood in front of me, one hand on a hip. "Do tell."

"Looks like I'm keeping you from a match. Heading to the club?"

She made an ugly noise in her throat and turned from me. She headed to the nearest chair and sat heavily on it. "I understood that Michael gave you your money. Why are you still here?"

I could see her bloodred fingernail polish from where I stood. Bloodred, like fully oxygenated blood. The kind that coursed once through Farley, Banks, and Cameron. Even Michael Martin, though more at some time than now.

"I gave the money back."

Her eyebrows went up in unison. "You did?" She realized that surprise wasn't the emotion she wanted to convey, and they came back down. "Why would you do that? Aren't you just in it for the cash?"

"Sure. That's why I pulled you out of Farley's place. That's why I got the dirty pictures of you back."

"I didn't mean to imply that you haven't been very helpful."

"No, you didn't think about any of that. You're just being a bitch. You think you're a hard-ass. But you're just a grade-B bitch."

"Now see here..."

"Yeah." I found the other chair and sat across from her before she could stand up and really get going "I know. Imogene doesn't take this kind of crap from anyone. Right? You quit taking Martin's crap a while ago. Right?"

Her eyes were large and empty.

"You knew about the horse. Banks told you."

"You don't know what you're talking about."

I lit a cigarette and let the end of it burn. The smoke made its way halfway to Imogene then stopped. Even smoke refused to get too close.

"Maybe not. But bear with me. This is good."

I took in a lungful of smoke and exhaled.

"Farley had the goods on Banks and Rex. He had the goods on Abbie too. But he started with Banks. That's where the real blackmail would happen. Martin wouldn't like that, would he? A jockey playing both ends against the middle, so to speak."

She pulled her impossibly white shoes up under her. Her long, tanned legs with their taut muscles gleamed as if they'd been oiled.

"And then Michael hires me, tells me to take care of Farley. Remember? You tried to pump me for information, but none came out. You wanted to know how much I knew."

"You didn't know anything. You told me that yourself."

"True. I didn't know anything then. But you told Farley anyway."

Her head snapped up.

"Please don't deny it, Imogene."

"You are so damn sure of yourself."

"And Farley told Peele, his landlord. You see, Peele was doing Michael's bidding. But you had your own game you wanted to play."

"That's not true."

"Of course it is. You and Farley had a nice little arrangement going. You were going to bleed your husband as dry as you could. Blackmail. The bets. The whole nine yards. And you would run away with Banks."

She was quiet now. She didn't look at me. She didn't look anywhere but down.

"You hadn't counted on Farley being willing to bleed him with pictures of you. You hadn't counted on your husband being willing to sacrifice a jockey. Maybe you didn't know he was going to sacrifice the horse. I think you completely underestimated how ruthless the old drunk could be." I laughed, but not at her. I laughed at how even the smart ones aren't that smart. "Farley and Martin and Banks. They all got over on you."

When she finally answered, her voice was smaller. "When Richard disappeared, I was afraid something had happened to him. But then, the rumor was that he'd taken off with Vera Peele." Her mouth made a tiny movement, corners turned downward in disgust. "What a joke."

"I don't know. Vera is attractive enough."

"Don't be stupid. Why would he take off with a horse trainer's wife?"

"When he could have had the horse owner's wife?"

Her mouth tightened into a knot.

"Why indeed? When I checked with the police, and they knew about Vera but not about you, that's when I realized your little fling with Banks was a complete secret. Except to you and your husband. If Peele had known, Spatz would have taken care of you too."

Color came to her cheeks and then drained. "I don't think so." But she didn't sound like she meant it. She sounded like she'd just thought of it.

"Think about it. They killed Banks because he knew about the horse. And then, they killed the horse." I took another drag. "Honey, if they'd known you knew about the horse, you'd be as dead as the rest of them."

She exhaled as if she was smoking herself. "I don't think you have any idea how you bore me."

"That's too bad. Your husband thinks the world of me. He'd like to keep me around forever."

I saw her throat tighten then swallow. "Why is that?"

"Because I know everything. And I know that it's not Peele and Spatz that are the real movers here. Your husband is. He's the prime mover. The first cause. The one behind it all."

That was when it hit her fully. It wasn't that I knew the scam. That I knew the scammer. And that she should have known.

She rearranged herself on the chair. She was a little older than my taste, but she did have the knack. She sat in a manner that was seductive and classy at the same time. Like an old Ava Gardner movie. "That might not be a bad idea after all. Keeping you around. I might eventually get used to you."

I took one last drag and sank the butt in the very last bit of coffee in her cup. It made a pathetic sizzle before it went out. "That's where you're wrong. I wouldn't like you to get used to me any more than I'd like to get used to you. You people make me sick."

"I bet you'd get well quickly if you had enough cash."

"You'd lose that bet, Imogene." I took the coffee cup from her and put it on the chair's arm. It balanced but just barely. "I told Martin that I'd keep the secret. It's not my game to play. He may get Peele off if he hires the right lawyer and greases the right judge. So there's no real percentage for me to shoot off my mouth, given that I could do that, and everybody would be mad at me."

"So why not just take the money? I would."

"You already took the money. And you know what?"

"What?"

"That's the problem I'm trying to avoid. Ending up like you."

I took one last look before I left. Imogene, in her impossibly white outfit and beautifully tanned legs, looking confused by the appearance of somebody who didn't give a damn about the amount of money being offered just to keep his mouth shut. Me, walking away from a sweet payday that I wouldn't ever see again, just for doing nothing. A cigarette, soaking up brown liquid into the filter tip, inside a coffee cup, balanced on the arm of a chair.

I got myself outside the house as fast as I could, before the cup fell off the chair and before I could change my mind.

Chapter 37

Tʜᴀᴛ ɴɪɢʜᴛ, ᴀғᴛᴇʀ ᴇᴠᴇʀʏᴛʜɪɴɢ got all sorted out, I called up the medical examiner and let him know what had come out in the wash.

"No way. I wouldn't have figured that."

"Yeah. That's what everyone said. Even I said that."

I called a number and asked for James Lee Penny. Could have been Ronnie. But maybe not. James Lee had a whole mob working for him. It might have been my spotter, Reese Lockman.

When James Lee came to the phone, I thanked him.

"Glad it all worked out."

"But James Lee? The Sandman. How did you know to connect that dot?"

"I didn't know, kid. I just asked myself, who do I know that would know about horses getting bumped off? It's not a usual thing, you know? But where you've got a horse owner with money problems, you'll usually find somebody desperate."

"I guess."

"Hey, you ever hear that old saying? Never buy a boat. It's nothing but trouble. What you want is to have a friend with a boat. All the pleasure. None of the pain."

"So?"

"Same with owning racehorses. Better just to watch them run, bet a little here and there."

James Lee had made his bets, it seemed. They seemed to be paying off. For now. "Stay healthy, man."

The voice at the other end laughed. "That's the goal. That's always the goal. Without your health, you don't have anything."

Then I called Anson. "Tomorrow night, meet me at the country club. Let's have our talk out there."

"I didn't realize you were a member."

I'm not. Special dispensation."

"Okay, but in the dining room? Isn't that a little public?"

"We won't be in the dining room. We'll be out in the paddock area."

***

We stood shoulder to shoulder, or at least as close to that as I can with a guy who's that much shorter than I am. Jet Pack had been relocated to the stables at the hunt club, and Kid Galahad had been pulled from the sweepstakes and was on his way back to Florida. Without horses, I realized, a stable is just a drafty barn.

"That's a lot to process." Anson scratched his beard. It was a therapist kind of thing to do, the way he did it. Slow. Thoughtful. Probably done for my benefit. When I didn't respond, he asked, "How do you feel about all of it?"

"I'm glad it went the way it did. I probably couldn't have proved it."

"At the very least, you took quite a chance. That poor horse could have been dead. And how would you have looked?"

"There was never any danger of that. Simms and I were out there the night before. We bypassed the outlet. There was no juice there at all."

He scratched his beard again. "I see."

The back of the stall was open, and the moonlight spilled onto Fool's Trade's straw. Clean straw for a dead horse. There were things I never would understand about the business.

"You were sure, then?"

"I was sure. It was the only way it could have happened."

Without a notepad, Anson drew circles in the dirt with his shoe. "But no one else believed that. How does that make you feel?"

"How does what make me feel?"

Another circle with his toe then another with his heel. "Being right. When everyone else was wrong."

"Everyone else wasn't wrong. They just weren't looking."

"You feel nothing? Not even a little vindication?" He leaned on the stable door, drew a line in the dirt.

"Does that not seem normal?"

"Let me ask the questions, okay?"

"Okay."

We stood there, him asking questions and me not answering them. I didn't have any answers.

"How about this one? Are you going back to the police academy?"

"Flood told me I'd have to pay Metro back if I didn't go."

"Then you're staying."

"No. I'm looking for money."

The rest of our session was unremarkable. He tried to get me to talk about how I felt, and I tried to tell him what I did and what I knew. I wasn't feeling a lot, and I was certain that would open a whole vein of questions for him. And I wasn't up for it. Not tonight.

"Why did you invite me here, Jackson? You clearly don't want to talk, but you wanted me to see this place. Is there some significance in that?"

"You're the shrink. You tell me."

"It's not my job to know what's on your mind. It's your job."

He was right. "Then I can't do my job."

***

I sat on an overturned washtub, smoking one cigarette after another, until I was interrupted by the sound of shoes padding softly toward the barns. Loafers, I thought. Worn by somebody who usually strides forward but who is trying to walk quietly. It's a game I play. Usually, I'm wrong.

This time, I was right. Flood looked surprised when I looked up. "An elephant would have had a better chance of sneaking up on me."

"Hard to do on a quiet night. Out here. So far off the road you couldn't hear a siren if one went by."

"Which is why horses like it. Which is why I like it."

He crouched in front of me. "Nice work last night."

"I did the prep. You made the arrest."

"I did my job, which is to arrest the bad guys, bring them in so the system can start doing its job." He reached into his shirt pocket and took out a toothpick. It went in the left side of his mouth and immediately shifted to the right. "Could be your job too, Jackson. You're good at the hard parts, the parts no one can teach you."

"Must be the easy parts that trip me up, Flood."

"You're overthinking it. Start over with the new class at the academy. You'll fit in great."

Fit in great. The words echoed in my head for a second longer than I wanted them to. I could smell the straw, still fresh, in the stable and could see the moonlight reflected in the trough water.

It reminded me of a night in-country, many years before, and the straw was for a family's water buffalo and the moonlight was for the Viet Cong.

I was here and I was there, all of a sudden and all at the same time.

Flood was Flood, but he was also a smart-ass first lieutenant who'd been promoted out of his butter bars, and I was just a grunt, infantry, trying not to get used all the way up before they sent me home. "But you fit in great," he said. "We can use more like you. You're good at the hard parts."

Did Flood say that? Or did the LT say it, trying to get me to reenlist, take a second tour in the jungle? I realized it didn't matter. I wasn't going to the academy any more than I was going to reenlist. I wasn't part of a unit, and I wasn't any closer to finding my way.

I heard my voice. It sounded hollow, echoing in my ears. I didn't know if it was then, or if it was now.

"Sorry, Lieutenant. I got nothing."

Also By TJ Arant

For a free story about Jackson's start as a crime solver, head over to https://dl.bookfunnel.com/xe0cfwzxco for your free copy of *Trader*. You'll get a monthly newsletter with news and updates on coming books as well (I'll never spam you or sell your name; you hate people who do that as much as I do).

www.ingramcontent.com/pod-product-compliance
Lightning Source LLC
Chambersburg PA
CBHW021437150726
47989CB00001B/277